SASHA MARSHALL

Mistletoe WISHES

This is a work of fiction. Names, characters, places, and incidents are either the products of the author's imagination or are used fictitiously. Any resemblance to actual persons (living or dead), events, or locations is entirely coincidental.

Sasha Marshall Arts

Atlanta, GA

Copyright © 2023 by Sasha Marshall

Second Edition

Published in the United States of America.

All rights reserved. No part of this book may be reproduced in any form or by any electronic or mechanical means, including information storage and retrieval systems, without permission in writing from the publisher or author, except by a reviewer, who may quote brief passages in a review.

We at Sasha Marshall Arts enjoy hearing from readers.

Edited by: N-D Scribable Services

Cover Design: Sasha Marshall and Emily Davis

Interior Design: Michael Creamer

Happy readings!

Sasha Marshall

For Beth

Thank you for your undying love and support for the past three years. You are my favorite Vamptress. I couldn't do this without you. This book exists because of you.

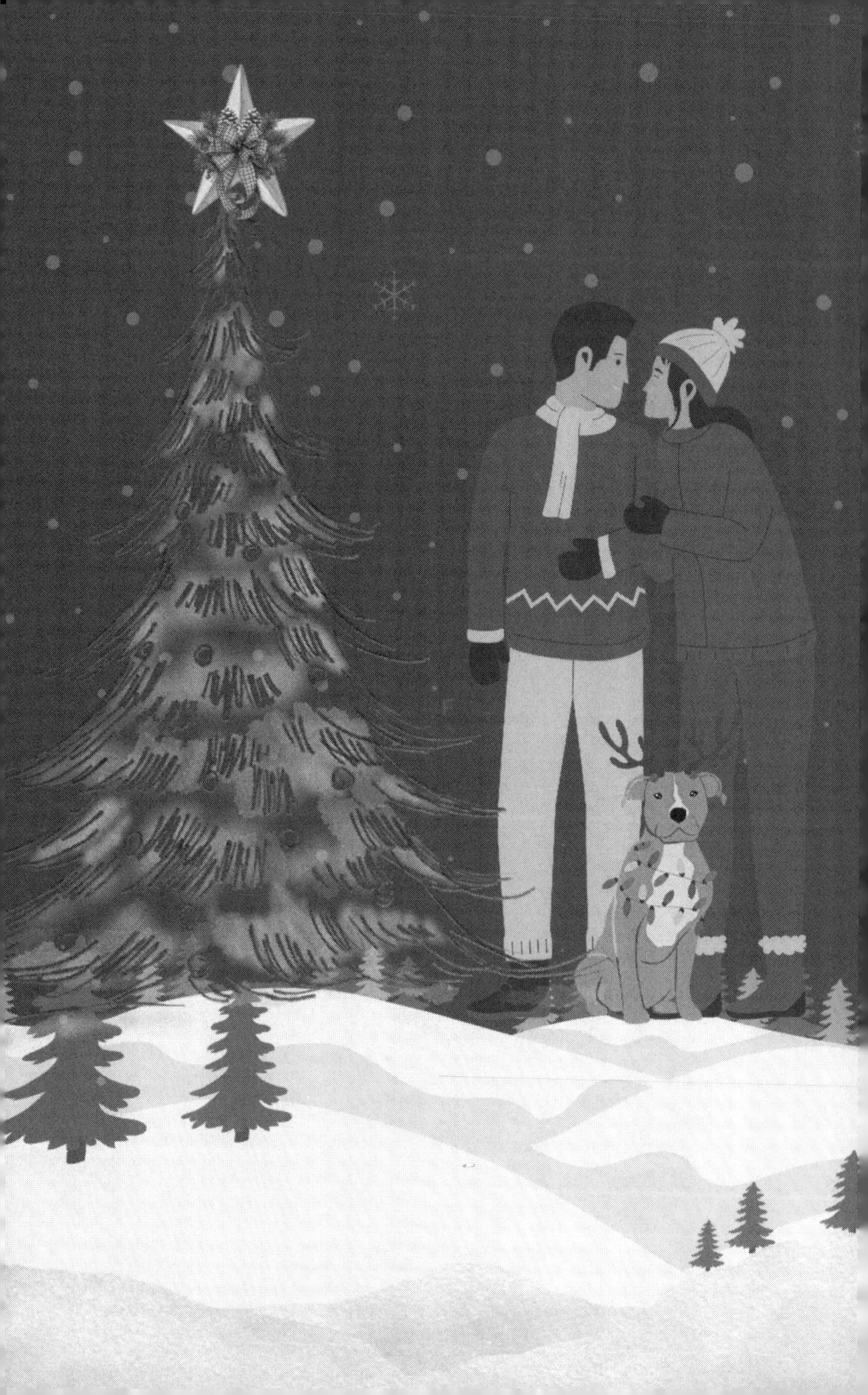

Prologue

Once upon a time, long ago, in a land far away... Well, actually it wasn't that far away, although Mistletoe Creek, Tennessee, often seems more off the beaten path where it lies nestled against the Smoky Mountain foothills. And it really wasn't so long ago. A few short months ago, the following conversation was overheard between Fern Myers, Fawn Carter, and Merry Andrews during their monthly meeting. When later asked, all three women would deny the conversation ever occurred.

"It's your deal, Fern," Merry says as she glances at the window when a colorful leaf drifts off the oak tree just outside.

Fern scoffs and stretches her fingers before picking the well-worn deck up off the shiny table.

"I *always* deal, Merry."

"More like always cheat," Fawn mumbles.

"Excuse me?" Fern adjusts her bifocals on the edge of her nose.

"I find it highly suspect that every time you deal, you also seem to win."

"If you want to deal..."

"I don't. But I do want you to play fair."

"Play fair? Just because I'm lucky doesn't mean I don't—"

"Ladies!" Merry jumps in before their argument can escalate.

It wouldn't be the first time a confrontation between the two of them had been stopped before it went beyond just words.

"I really don't feel like getting kicked out of here again by Mayor Anderson. We just got invited back. And personally, I didn't care for power walking all summer in the heat."

While the mansion of the original founder of Mistletoe Creek had been turned into a combination of public gathering spaces and city offices, the last time they'd flipped the table during a card game, Mayor Anderson had been left with no other option—he had banned all three septuagenarians for the entire summer.

"I did offer for us to play Yahtzee instead," Fawn says.

"We could always actually learn bridge instead of just telling everyone that's what we play," Merry adds.

"We've been playing Texas Hold 'Em for thirty years. Yahtzee is for when I babysit my grandkids. And if we told everyone we were playing poker instead of bridge, we'd have the entire town trying to join in our games." Fern levels a look at both of the other women until they nod.

The room is silent except for the crackle of cards as they swoosh across the table along with sighs and murmurs as each woman considers her cards.

"It's too quiet." Merry drops her cards face down.

"What do you mean?" Fern asks.

"It's been ages since we've had a wedding. Or any good gossip."

"We just went to Dawn and Jack Phillips's wedding two weekends ago. Raise ten." Fawn tosses a blue chip onto the small pile and the other two follow suit.

"It was a beautiful wedding." Merry sighs, a dreamy smile playing on her lips. "Even if Fawn fell asleep during the ceremony."

"You take that back, Merry Andrews! Or I'll tell Dawn that you didn't like the light pink of her wedding dress," Fawn fires back.

Merry's eyes narrow across the table. "You wouldn't."

Fawn crosses her arms. "Try me."

"Fine. You win. I take it back." Merry's voice is nothing more than a mumble. Fern sighs and glances between the two of them.

"I can't believe Dawn is all grown-up and married now," Fern says, trying to redirect the conversation. "I still remember when I used to babysit her."

"Such a good girl."

"I'm just glad that she and Jack finally found each other." Merry checks her bet and turns to Fawn.

"They wouldn't have if it wasn't for us," Fawn reminds the other two.

Both other women nod in agreement.

"I thought that was never going to happen no matter how many times we kept signing Dawn up to volunteer with Jack at Parks and Wildlife." Merry rolls her eyes.

Fawn shrugs. "They finally stopped fighting it."

"It was a beautiful wedding," Fern says.

"I already said that." Merry stares at Fawn.

"Who cares? It's still true."

"We need more weddings." Fawn checks her bet and Fern deals the last card.

"No one is close to dating, let alone marriage." Fern studies her cards in her hands before lifting her shrewd gaze to the five cards on the table.

"Neither were Dawn and Jack last year and look at them now. On their honeymoon." Merry clasps her hands together and the cards in her hand crinkle.

It wouldn't be the first deck to be lost to their lack of attention. And it definitely wouldn't be the last.

"So what are we going to do about it?" Fawn asks.

"Same thing we always do," Fern responds. "Let's see, there's Pierce and Hudson. Either of whom would be a catch."

"Don't forget Robyn or Elle. But not for either of those boys." Fawn taps her lip as she adds to the list.

"No, all four of them are ready for something special. Something spectacular. It's…" Fern's voice fades as her attention shifts back to her cards.

"It's matchmaking time," Merry says and gasps when Fawn pushes in all her chips.

"All in, ladies. Who's next?"

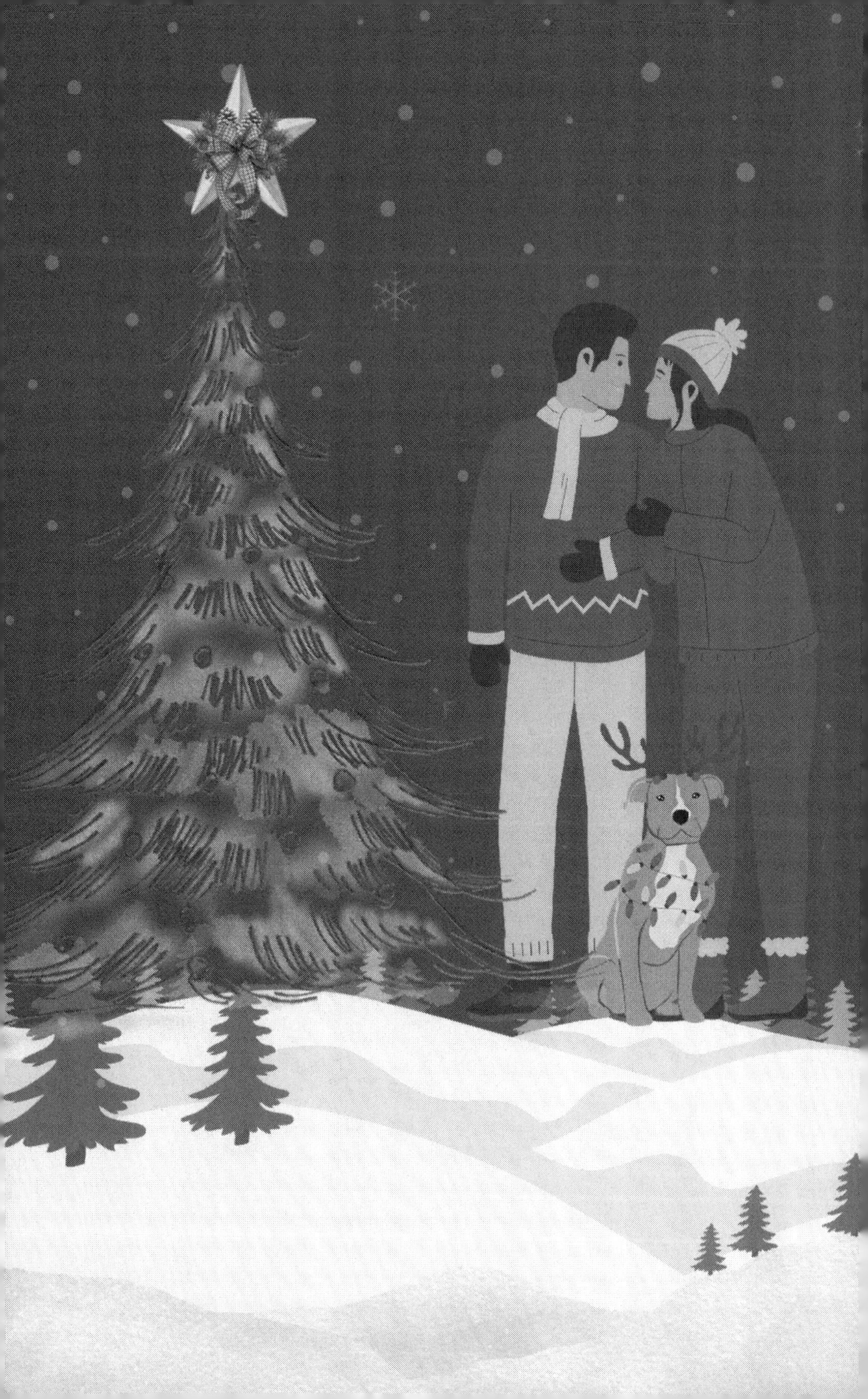

Chapter One
Stella

Sitting up straight as a board, I check the button on my black suit jacket once more for no other reason than to have a task to keep me busy. My leg bounces up and down, expending my nervous energy. Job interviews have to be the most nervewracking experience known to man. I do my best to focus on my resume, committing each date to memory in case I grow flustered during the process.

"Stella Black?" A graying woman with teased hair, sporting bright blue eyeshadow, smiles at me from the lobby door.

A sigh escapes me but does nothing to quell my anxiety. "Hi, that's me." I inwardly cringe, realizing how ridiculous I sound when I'm the only person here at seven in the morning. Reaching her, I extend my hand. "Stella."

Ugh.

Why are my palms so sweaty?

Gross.

I should've wiped them on my skirt.

"Pleasure," she says and is kind enough not to mention my wet handshake. "I'm Matilda. We spoke on the phone a few days ago."

"Nice to meet you in person." I incline my dark head.

"Thank you for agreeing to such an early meeting." She leads me from the plain and simple aesthetic of a typical small town legal office.

Past the lobby, the cream walls continue with unimpressive artwork hanging every few feet. I'm more accustomed to big city legal firms in Atlanta and Los Angeles displaying their wealth. I once again silently remind myself that Mistletoe Creek, Tennessee, isn't anywhere near a metropolis. It's exactly the change of pace and anonymity I need in my life.

Matilda arrives at an office two doors past a conference room. I immediately recognize it as her space. It's sunny and decorated with a slew of family pics, coloring pages taped to the wall, and notes written in crayon. It's easy to feel the love and light surrounding this woman.

She takes the office chair behind her desk and waves a hand at the armchair in front. "Please, sit."

"Thank you." I have a seat, smooth my black skirt down, and sit tall.

Matilda doesn't waste any time in starting the interview. "Your resume is impressive, Ms. Black. It says you hold a B.S. in criminal justice with experience in contracts?"

"Yes, ma'am, that's correct. I've been a paralegal for close to eight years now." Hopefully, I sound as confident as I feel in my skill set.

"Wonderful. When we spoke a few days ago, I mentioned the position is part-time paralegal work and part-time administrative assistant to Mr. Saint. You're overqualified for it, but Kashton could use someone like you to help him be his best self. The practice could take on more clients if he could focus more on what's important and less on housekeeping tasks."

"I understand and am happy to be considered for both." *There.* That sounds eager, but not overly so.

"Kash needs a strong, independent employee who can manage the office without being micromanaged by him or the other partner." She opens her mouth to say more but closes it before she can. "It begins today if you can manage it."

My words rush out so fast I don't even think about my reply. "Yes, ma'am. If offered the job, I can begin today."

She looks as though she might squeal, but instead, claps her hands together in satisfaction. "This has worked out well. I can walk you through a typical day from the very start of the morning. I feel less nervous about leaving my boy in your hands now that we've met."

"Oh? Is he your son?"

A warm expression passes over her face. "No, there's no relation. I was his father's secretary before Kashton inherited me and the practice. I'm sad to leave after knowing him for most of his life, but my kids and grandchildren need me.

I've struggled with the idea of retirement for two years, but it's time. I can leave him in your capable hands."

Matilda stands from her chair, retrieves her purse from one of the desk drawers, and walks out of the office. "Come on, Stella, let's go wake our boy."

It's adorable she's so affectionate toward a man she's known since he was a child. Without meeting him, I already know he's lucky to have her.

Leaving the cream walls and hideous artwork behind, she moves to my faded green Toyota Camry — the only other car in the lot. "We'll take your car."

Finding her request to use my car a bit odd, I reply with a smile and unlock the doors. "Sure."

Matilda almost gets us killed on the trek across Mistletoe Creek with her last-minute direction, but they eventually lead us to a quaint little neighborhood off the town square. It's filled with historic houses with wrap-around porches, rocking chairs, and white picket fences. The winter lawns are barer than I imagine them to be in warmer months, but I can tell they're usually manicured and landscaped. I imagine the evenings during summer months are filled with the sounds of children playing and neighbors laughing with each other after a long day at work.

It's a perfect, picturesque place for a happy couple, a golden retriever named Max, and two-point-five kids.

It's a modern-day Mayberry. I love everything about the vibe and energy here. I half expect Andy and Barney to walk across the street in their police uniforms.

Matilda directs me to park on the street in front of a two-story, white house with a red brick mailbox at the end of the drive. Noticing a boxwood wreath with a burlap ribbon hanging on the front door, I wonder if Mrs. Saint spends her days at home decorating her gorgeous house or if she's employed as well.

Following Matilda from the car to the drive, we stop at the front door. She digs a set of keys from her purse and sorts through the hundred or so hanging from the ring.

"Ah, here!" She grins as if she's won the lottery instead of locating a key.

Upon opening the door, a foul scent hits me right in the face, nearly doubling me over. Swallowing a gag, I force myself to breathe through my mouth to avoid barfing in front of my new boss. I hate my weak constitution.

Matilda blinks a few times at the smell, but she forges ahead like a Viking warrior, who is unconcerned with what could possibly create such a putrid odor. I'm more than a little worried we might find Mr. Saint no longer of the breathing variety.

"Kashton!" she shouts from the foyer, but there's no answer. A huge sigh comes from her direction. "Someone had too much fun this weekend," she mumbles under her breath. "Kash!"

A groan and a thud come from the room on the other side of the foyer. We make our way over there and push through a swinging door. The older woman comes to a halt in front of me.

I run into the back of her, step around, and apologize for not paying attention. "I'm so sor..."

My mouth drops open as the scene unfolds in front of me. Pink zebra print panties dangle from the kitchen light fixture. Tequila bottles, limes, and a small mountain of salt cover the large island in the middle of the room. A brunette, three shades lighter than my dark brown hair, is asleep and sprawled across the kitchen table clad in only her birthday suit. Two other naked women are passed out in kitchen chairs and slumped over the table face down. I hope at least one of them is Mrs. Saint.

But it's the tall, naked, backside of the nicest male specimen I've ever seen standing in front of the open dishwasher, relieving himself inside the appliance, that stuns my mouth shut and forces my words to disappear. Do men really look like that?

Matilda crosses her arms over her chest. "Kash, you're pissin' in the dishwasher."

The urinating man grunts but continues his task.

I lean over to the current secretary and whisper, "Um, is he okay?"

She shoots a tight smile in my direction. "Kash needs direction sometimes. He forgets what day it is every now and then."

Her forced smile drops when she marches across the kitchen and slaps the man's behind so hard, it leaves a bright red handprint across his perfect ass.

"Ow! Stop it, Matty!" Kash shouts at her over his shoulder.

Without a word, she moves over to the woman lying across the table and slaps her on the ass too. "Time to go, ladies. The fun is over." She raises her nose in the air and sniffs. "Has anyone in this room showered recently?"

The woman groans, but the two in the chairs don't make a peep.

Matilda goes over to the kitchen sink, and starts filling a glass pitcher with cold water, humming a nice tune while she waits. When it's full, she returns to the table and pours the contents on the woman's face, who wakes with a start and swallows half the pitcher. She nearly drowns from it as a garbled slew of profanities follows, with her choking back the liquid.

"What the fuck?" She sits straight up on the table with wide eyes and a drenched head.

Matilda's hands go to her hips, and her head cocks to the side. "Bless your heart, honey."

I don't bother to hide my smirk at the thinly veiled insult.

"Time to slither back home, sweethearts." Matilda slides around the table to another woman passed out face down, picking her head up by the nape. "You too."

"It's Sunday, Matty!" Kash's delayed protest booms through the room, his gravelly voice climbing up my spine and warming my blood.

Turning my attention back to him, I discover he's turned around. I choke on my own spit when I see the large, flaccid dick swinging between his legs.

Can a limp cock still be that big?

"My eyes are up here, gorgeous," he says, amusement coloring his deep voice.

I admit, I have to force my gaze from his impressive crotch and lock my green eyes on his blues. Something happens in the next few moments — it's almost like I've been here before — deja vu. But I know without a doubt, I've never seen or met Kashton Saint. He's not a man you'd forget, especially if the first view happens to be of his marvelously tattooed, naked body. He's not at all the older attorney I expected to find.

"Does she speak?" he asks Matilda, his eyes dancing down my body.

"I suppose I should've warned her about the full details of the job and your *active* lifestyle." She turns to me. "Forgive me. Nothing shocks me anymore with this one."

My mouth opens, but nothing escapes.

How in the world do I respond to this … *fuckery*?

There's not a handbook I can consult in this situation.

"She's mute," Kash says, his sleepy eyes raking over me again.

"You're standing in the middle of your kitchen with your ding-a-ling swinging between your legs, you big dummy. You've scared her half to death with that thing." Matilda chides him like he's still the teen boy she referred to earlier.

Kash's response surprises me. He looks down at his rather large appendage and checks it out as if offended by my offense. "What's wrong with Jack?"

The woman from the table moseys over to him, throws her arm around his waist, and leans in for a kiss.

Kash pulls back, avoiding lip contact with her. "Nuh-uh, you know the rules. No kissing, kitten." He slaps her on the ass and grins down at her from his tall height, before spinning her around by the shoulders and showing her the door. "Time to go. Matty's here."

Confusion spreads across kitten's face, but she leaves the kitchen, hopefully searching for her clothes. All this nudity is making me uncomfortable.

Kash takes his eyes off her ass when she leaves the room and settles his gaze back on me. He steps across the room with his hand extended out for a handshake and a smile firmly on his face. "Kashton Saint. It's nice to meet you. So you'll be replacing Matty?"

The most difficult thing I've ever had to overcome in my twenty-nine years is managing *not* to look down at King Ding-a-ling's dick when he steps right in front of me. His hand is just above the anaconda. I'm semi-scared the damn thing will strike out and bite me.

"Stella Black." The words finally come out, but they sound like someone else. I must still be in shock from being visually assaulted with the biggest pecker I've ever seen in real life.

One of the women from the chairs moves in our direction, her dark hair sticking up and out in every which way as if someone fisted it.

Oh.

Ohhhh.

He likes to pull hair.

I will not think about this man pulling my hair. I will not think about this man pulling my hair. I will not think about this man pulling my hair.

Heat creeps into my cheeks, showing off my discomfort to the entire room.

I remind myself how much I need this job. I need somewhere just like Mistletoe Creek to lie low, but a girl has to eat while she hides.

"Nice to meet you," I add, hoping I sound more convincing to him than I do to myself.

His blue eyes travel across my face, pausing on each feature for a long moment before moving on.

"Likewise." He hasn't stopped pumping my hand up and down in our handshake.

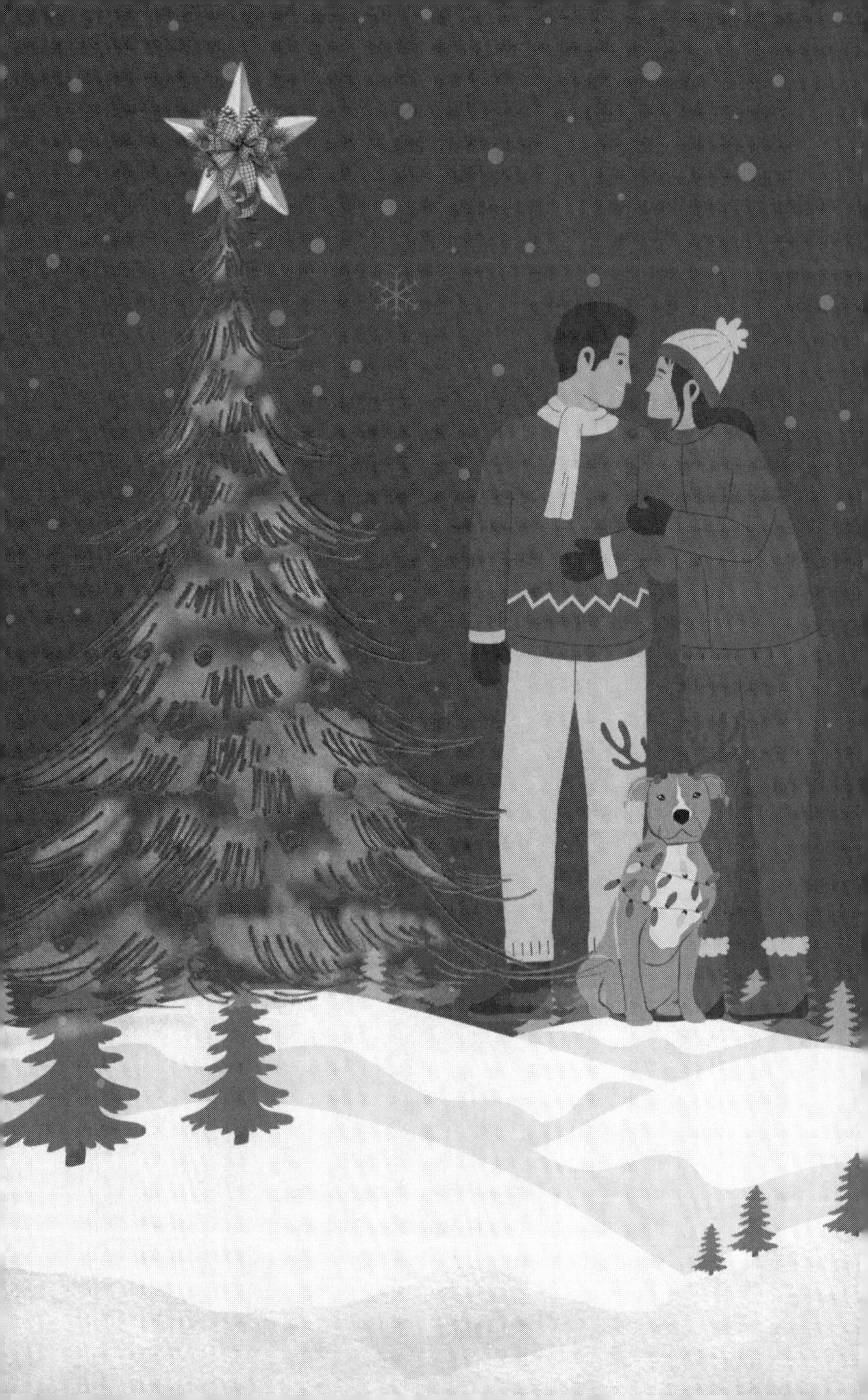

Chapter Two
Kash

I'm staring into the most exquisite green eyes I've ever seen, shaking her hand like an excited car salesman. Dropping it, I back away and suddenly remember I'm naked as the day I was born, and her hand was so close to my dick I could feel its warmth. Maybe it was just wishful thinking though.

Damn, she's gorgeous. I bet she'd be even prettier with her legs pushed behind her head.

If I could just clear the fog from my cocaine and alcohol-riddled brain to remember her name, this would go a lot smoother.

A whooshing sound precedes sugar hitting plastic. Except, it's *not* sugar. Spinning around, I discover Matty sweeping thousands of dollars of grade A blow into the trash can.

"Matty, no! That's not trash!" I cover my eyes at the atrocity occurring right in front of them.

I cast a look across the room at the brunette in the black skirt and jacket. She arches a brow, shooting her gaze at the pile of white powder amongst the tequila bottles. Matilda probably thinks it's salt.

My secretary touches her tongue to the white residue left behind on her fingers before I can stop her. "It's not salt." The disappointment is evident in her voice.

Matty and the gorgeous woman both shoot me unpleasant expressions. Yikes, I haven't felt this small since my pops was alive.

So, I do what I always do in this situation and use my sparkling personality to win over the crowd. "Has anyone told either of you ladies how pretty y'all are this morning? The beauty emanating from both of you is absolutely ethereal."

Judging by their unimpressed expressions, I'll have to do a better job of convincing them. Since my synapses aren't properly firing this morning, I scratch my head while I wait for the next genius move to flitter into my mind.

The remaining playmate of mine lounges at the table, watching us like a tennis match, appearing incredibly confused by the conversations taking place in my kitchen. I'm glad to know it's not only me who isn't using their frontal lobe quite yet.

"What time is it?" the woman asks, looking at all three of us for an answer.

I wish for the life of me I could remember whether her name is Tiffany or Arlene, not that it matters. She wasn't memorable or worthy of a repeat performance.

The hot brunette in the skirt checks her smart watch with disapproval heavy in her words. "Fifteen past eight."

My playmate takes her time outwardly computing the information. It takes her a long minute. "Thanks." She leaves the dining chair and walks through the kitchen.

When she reaches us, she stops in her tracks with wide eyes. Her hand flies to her mouth as she rushes past me to the kitchen sink and barfs. The mixed aroma of tequila and vomit fills my nose. It's never a pleasant combination.

An odd sound squeaks from across the room. At first, I think it's Matilda having a fucking stroke or heart attack, but she's focused on the brunette goddess.

"Stella, are you all right, dear?" Matty starts for her.

Stella — that's her name — so perfect and feminine for the woman it belongs to.

I move my gaze back to her. She's ghostly pale and green around the gills, but I'd still fuck her right here and right now. She's classy – not my usual type. A chuckle escapes me at the mere thought of my taste in women, which are beautiful and easy. There's no way I could ever put her in a room with the females I ruin on a weekly basis.

My new secretary gags with her mouth open, and the sound spilling from it reminds me of a dog throwing up. It doesn't belong anywhere near this beauty.

I rush over to her, arriving at the same time as Matilda, who places a soothing hand on Stella's shoulder. The brunette at the sink continues to vomit quite loudly, causing Stella to close her eyes and gag again.

This isn't good. She's going to ...

The stunning Stella bends at the waist and pukes all over me, the trajectory of the warm liquid hitting me square in the cock before dripping from the tip of it and splattering around my feet. I blame my shock for not moving out of her way until she's done a few minutes later. I've never seen a woman upchuck so much.

A small smile threatens to spread into a wide grin across Matilda's face as she checks on a now upright Stella, but Matty's stare remains on me. "Oh, my. You've had a terrible first day."

While warm regurgitated food continues to drip off my dick, a pair of hands reaches around me from behind, planting on either side of my chest. "Oh, shit, Bunny, she puked on you."

Matilda quirks a brow at the nickname and mouths, "Bunny?". Her expression indicates she's not a fan of the pet name or the woman.

"I think I should go home and lie down. Can you find a ride back to the office?" Stella only addresses Matty while she gives me the cold shoulder.

She's upset, but I can't figure out why. I didn't make her puke. Her gag reflex isn't my fault, and yet, it bothers me that she's avoiding eye contact with me.

"Sure, dear! We understand. You've had a rough introduction, but tomorrow is a new day!" Matilda is never this damn cheerful.

I don't understand. I puke a few times a week, depending on my alcohol consumption the night before, but I still manage to make it to work ... at some point during the day.

"It's nice to meet you." I extend my hand to her, her breakfast still sliding down my legs.

She finally swings her gaze in my direction, but she looks at my ear. "Yes."

Without another word, she turns on her heel and ambles out the way she came. By the time I focus on Matty, her hands rest on her hips with a pissed off expression.

Again, I feel small.

Tiffany or Arlene wiggles at my back and lays her head against my skin, which immediately crawls from her affection. I don't need love. I need sex.

Unwrapping her hands from around my middle, I disengage and take two long steps past Matty, knowing she'll take care of her for me.

"Where are you going?" Matilda is the closest thing to a mom I've had in thirty-five years.

Peering over my shoulder at her, I gesture at my crotch. "I need a shower after *your* girl puked on me." It came out harsher than I intended.

"Bunny, aren't you going to invite me?" Tiffany or Arlene whines.

"No. I've been puked on enough for one day." I turn the corner and take the stairs to my bedroom two at a time, looking forward to warm water ridding me of this stench.

Once I'm in my bathroom, I turn on the shower and wait until it warms up to my preference. When it's hotter than most people can stand it, I step underneath the waterfall. I wash the vomit from my body twice and shampoo my hair. As I'm washing it out, I'm hit in the face with cold water. There's a pause before I'm hit again with another wave of freezing liquid.

"What the fuck?!!" My eyes fly open and discover Matilda outside the shower holding two empty pitchers.

It's not my smartest move in history, because the shampoo stings my eyes, forcing them shut. They burn like the dickens, so I rub the hell out of them, prying them open for warm water to flush both out.

"I'm going blind, Matty!" I shout at her.

The clear, plastic pitcher flies into the shower and bops me upside the head.

"Listen, and listen really good, Kashton, because I'm leaving. Your desperate attempt this morning at getting rid of my replacement won't work in your favor. I've given you and your father decades of my life. My family needs me more than you do. I'm not going to stick around while you slowly drown yourself in booze, drugs, and women anyhow. I'm old, damn it. I wanted to start my retirement two years ago!

"I need you to get your shit together. You're a grown man for Christ's sake! Stop acting like you're twenty, pull it together, and grieve your father like a man. Today is my last day. God willing, your stunt this morning won't scare off Stella. If it does, it becomes your problem bright and early in the morning. I found you the best replacement in all of Tennessee. If you mess it up, it'll be your responsibility to fix it."

I blink water and shampoo out of my eyes. "You can't leave until I have another replacement."

She huffs. "You're an entitled shit, Kashton. This is my fault. I've coddled you since you were a teenager because your father was too hard on you. For the past two years, I've babied you like you're a toddler because your grief is complicated. You loved your father, but he was a hard man to love. I get it. So, let's understand one another from this day forward. You're lashing out at the world because you're in pain. Well, I'm not going to stand by and watch it any longer. It's time to grow up, Kash. And stop treating women like they're disposable after you've had your way with them. They're people too. While you're at it, put the booze down and stop putting things up your nose. Try going to work five days a week for a minimum of forty hours. You're a good attorney when you want to be."

She closes the door, leaving me with my mouth hanging wide open. I rush through the remainder of my shower and dress in a hurry. I call out for Matilda to beg her to stay for another week. I can't be left on my own at the practice. I'll drown within hours.

"Matty!"

There's no response. I guess she's giving me the silent treatment now. I know I crossed a line this morning, once again not being prepared for my work week, or anything other than making myself feel better.

"Matilda!"

I growl when she still doesn't reply, and like a chump, I search the entire house, sunroom, and back yard.

"Hello?"

Moving back through my home, I locate my cell on the kitchen counter, covered in Tiffany or Arlene's puke. I pull at my hair in frustration. "Goddamnit, Matty."

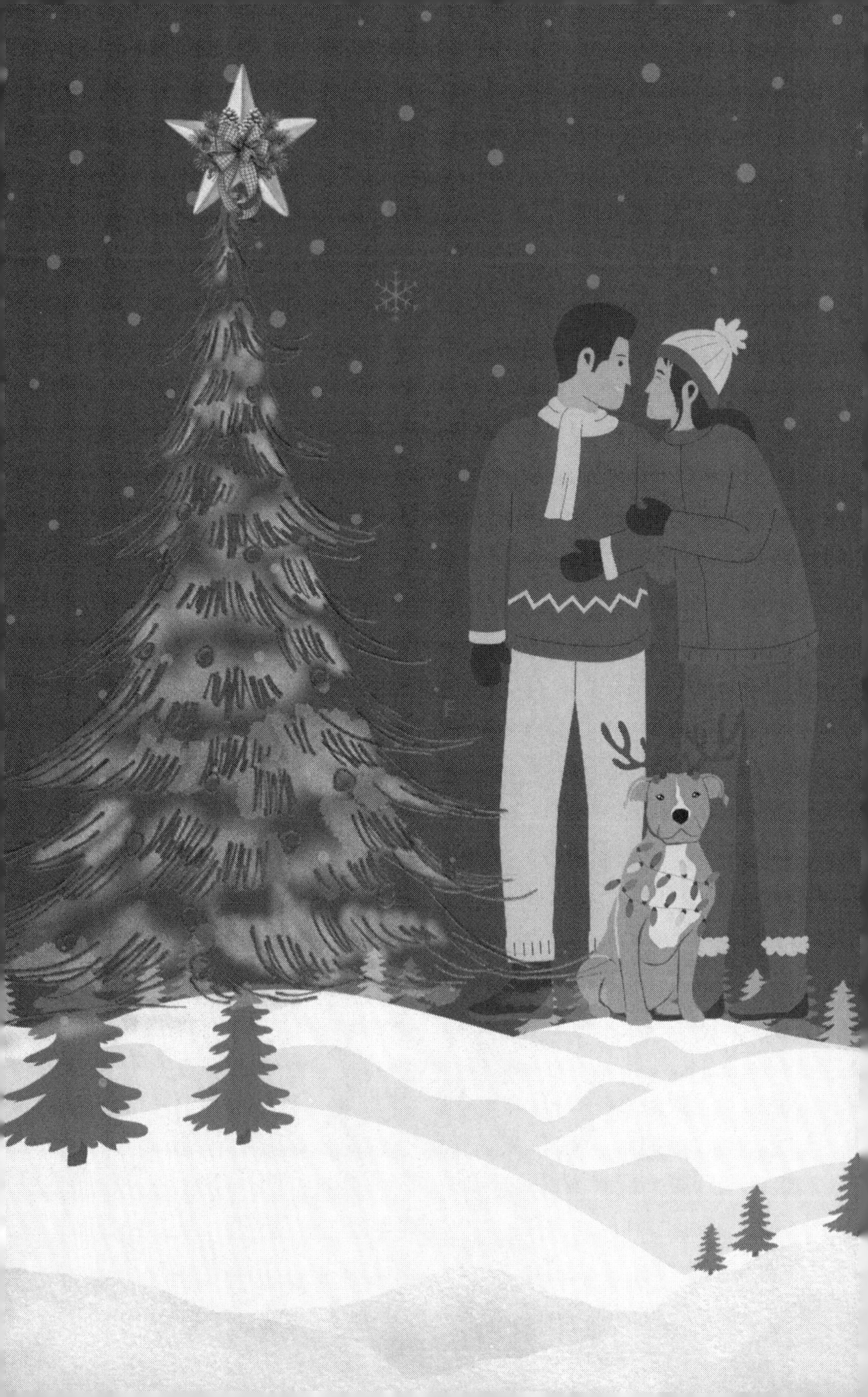

Chapter Three

Stella

I'd been sitting on the edge of the motel bed, staring at the dirty wall, for close to four hours when the manager of the joint knocks. It's his day to come by, looking for my weekly rent. There has to be another job in this small town. I'm a fast study, quick-witted, and college educated.

I should go down to the Mistletoe Creek Cafe once Gerald slithers back to his office on the other side of the Mistletoe Lodge property. I'm sure the cafe has a position on the night shift, which suits me fine. There will be less people to interact with. I'm also hoping to avoid local citizens asking questions I might not be prepared to answer at a moment's notice.

"Ms. Black! I saw you go inside your room earlier. If your rent isn't paid within the next hour, I'll have to phone the sheriff's department to evict you from the premises." His voice is raspy like he's smoked two packs of cigarettes a day for forty years.

I think he's going away, but then his slow creepy voice filters to my side of the door. "Are you ready to be a good girl for Daddy?"

The twisted laugh that follows incites my stomach to turn. Bile rises, but I swallow hard to fight the need to vomit again.

After the fiasco at Mr. Saint's house, I'm not going to be able to ask for the advance I was desperately hoping for - at a position I wasn't even sure I'd be hired for. I refuse to work for a man like Kashton Saint. If an attorney can't find his way to work on time each day without being treated like he's an adolescent, then I don't know how to help him. I'm not his mother.

Sighing, I look up at the ceiling, containing a brown water stain on the dingy, brown-speckled surface. I have to decide whether to use the last forty dollars in my pocket to eat for two days or keep this room another night. I could sleep in my car, but if I'm caught and my car's license plate is logged into the system, my location will reach Darren. All my careful steps and work over the past month will have been for naught.

Gerald continues to talk through the door, telling me all the explicit things he'd like to do to me. I'd have to drink an entire bar before I would ever be able to touch that pervert.

I'm lost in thought when a loud thud is followed by gurgling. A different masculine voice comes from the other side of the door. Another two low sounds hit the wood.

With wide eyes, I march across the room and peek through the peephole. There's so much movement on the other side that I'm unable to make out the newcomer for a long moment.

A cry for help goes out which sounds a lot like Gerald. Without thinking it through, I open the door and come face to face with familiar blue eyes.

Kashton Saint.

He stands over a cowering Gerald and repeatedly slaps him in the cheek.

"What else, Gerry?"

"I won't bother any other women." The manager is a blubbering mess with a bright red face.

Patting him harder than he should, Mr. Saint smiles down at Gerald. "That's great, Gerry." He reaches around the short, stocky manager with balding, dark hair in the shape of a horseshoe and plucks his wallet from his back pocket. Removing the man's driver's license, he recites the address listed on the front, taps the side of his head, and grins. "I know exactly where to find you, if need be. Don't let me get wind that you violated our little agreement, yeah?"

"What are you doing here?" My hands fly to my hips.

Kash straightens to his full, impressive height and winks at me. "Ah, it looks like I'm saving you from this shithead. It seems he's rather keen on sticking his cock in anything that moves, but from what I heard upon arriving, he is especially smitten with you." He hooks his thumb over his shoulder, pointing to the crying idiot. "You can say, 'Thank you', or did I overstep?"

Moving my gaze over to Gerald, I almost lie, but I don't want the weasel to think I'm easy or one to lie about his nasty treatment of women. "No, I was actually just leaving."

I rush inside, grab my packed luggage, and wheel them toward the door. Mr. Saint is just inside the door, looking nowhere near the disheveled King Ding-a-ling I happened upon this morning, but more like a GQ model with great skin, clear eyes, and white teeth. He certainly doesn't appear to be hungover from sex, drugs, and booze. It's impressive how he's put himself together in the span of four hours.

Itching from the bed bugs I imagine are all over this room, I whirl past him. Gerald is attempting to get himself off the floor, but he's struggling with his short Tyrannosaurus Rex arms and stumpy legs. I've never shown any type of inclination for violence, but I make an exception. Using the sole of my shoe, I place it on his ass and push him face down again.

Mr. Saint's husky laugh booms from behind me. "I like it! You've got moxie!"

He may have saved me from a creeper, but I don't like him much either. I lost my breakfast because of his bullshit. None of this would've happened if he'd been ready for work like a responsible freaking adult.

"Ugh." I leave my thoughts at that, turn on my heel, and march toward my car a few feet away.

Clicking my key fob, I pop the trunk, and throw my luggage in the back. When I close the back lid, I find Mr. Saint leaning against the driver's door, grinning like a lunatic.

"What do you want, Mr. Saint?" I ask in a terse tone.

"Call me Kash. I want *you*, Ms. Black. Please give me another chance to interview you myself. After reviewing your resume, which Matilda left on my desk, I concur with her — you're a perfect fit for the position. But I'd like to have a conversation while we're both wearing clothes." He winks one sparkling blue eye again, as if the clusterfuck this morning wasn't a big deal.

"Is there something in your eye?" I raise both my brows.

One is never supposed to see their boss naked. *Ever*. It defies the laws of the Universe for two people to be able to pretend they don't know what the other looks like nude. I can't possibly work for a man I've seen rocking out with his cock out, and I also can't forget what he nor his pecker look like.

"I can't work for you," I add, hoping he doesn't grow dramatic or drag this out.

A frown tugs at his handsome face. "Why the fuck not?"

I just go with the truth instead of making up an elaborate lie. "I've seen you without clothes."

His disenchantment grows deeper. "What's that have to do with anything?"

I throw my hands up, so completely over this day. "I'll always be imagining what you look like under your clothes."

The frown turns upside down as pure mischief fills his eyes. "Oh yeah? Tell me more."

I hold a finger up as if conducting the symphony of thoughts that roll off my tongue, but pause before I can deliver the twenty reasons I can think of not to be employed by him. "No. I'm not doing this with you. Get out of my way."

"Where are you going?" He's inquisitive like a child.

"Mistletoe Creek Cafe, if you must know." I huff as I speed-walk across the parking lot.

"Yes, I must know. I should go with you. I owe you breakfast after that horrible accident this morning anyhow." Opening my car door, he waves me to take my seat behind the wheel. "I'll follow you over. I know Dina, the owner. She fries the meanest chicken in Mistletoe Creek."

Deciding it's easier to appease him now and veer off elsewhere on my way to the cafe, I sigh and agree. "Okay. I'll meet you there."

He narrows his eyes at me for a long beat, shaking his head in disagreement. "Nah, I'll ride with you. I don't want to lose your trail just yet."

I don't bother hiding my eye roll. "Whatever. Let's go."

"Not so fast." He holds a hand up to stop me, turning his palm up. "I'll drive. I don't want you driving me to Bumfuck, Egypt and leaving me to find my own way home."

I shrug, not denying that I had a similar fleeting thought, but I square my shoulders — determined not to let him take my keys.

"This will go a lot easier for you if you willingly hand them over." It's difficult to determine if the playful tug at the corner of his mouth is taunting me to resist him or if the half smirk just perpetually graces his stupidly handsome face.

The standoff is only going to lead to physical touching between us. After seeing his anaconda this morning, I'm still semi afraid it'll bite me. I throw the keys at his face.

The graceful jackass snags them out of the air before they reach him. "Good choice, Ms. Black."

"Stella," I mumble under my breath.

Mr. Saint crosses the front of my car in a hurry, reaching my door before me and opening it. "Allow me."

I want to smack the smirk right off his face, but I incline my head in a silent thanks instead and climb inside. Kash closes the door, runs back around my Camry, and slides into the driver's seat. He gazes around the car, judging its old interior. At least it smells like Pina colada. It could be worse.

"Where's your car?" I think to ask, peering through the back windshield for an import, judging him right back for being a snooty little shit.

"There's not enough room in my car for your luggage," he points out, turning the ignition over and throwing the car in reverse.

He guns the accelerator and backs out of the parking space so fast I'm pretty sure he gives me whiplash. I grab onto the oh-shit-bar attached to the ceiling to keep myself from ending up in his lap.

"Would you mind slowing it down a little?" I need a bag to breathe into before I hyperventilate ... or puke, which I'd be okay with if it landed on him again.

I rush to buckle my seatbelt as he pulls out onto the highway in front of the motel. He punches the gas again and drives like a bat out of hell the entire four miles to the town limits where we arrive at Mistletoe Creek Cafe.

"I bet you're starving," he says from the driver's seat, completely oblivious to my impending heart attack.

I shoot him an "eat shit and die" look and pray I lose my lunch in his lap.

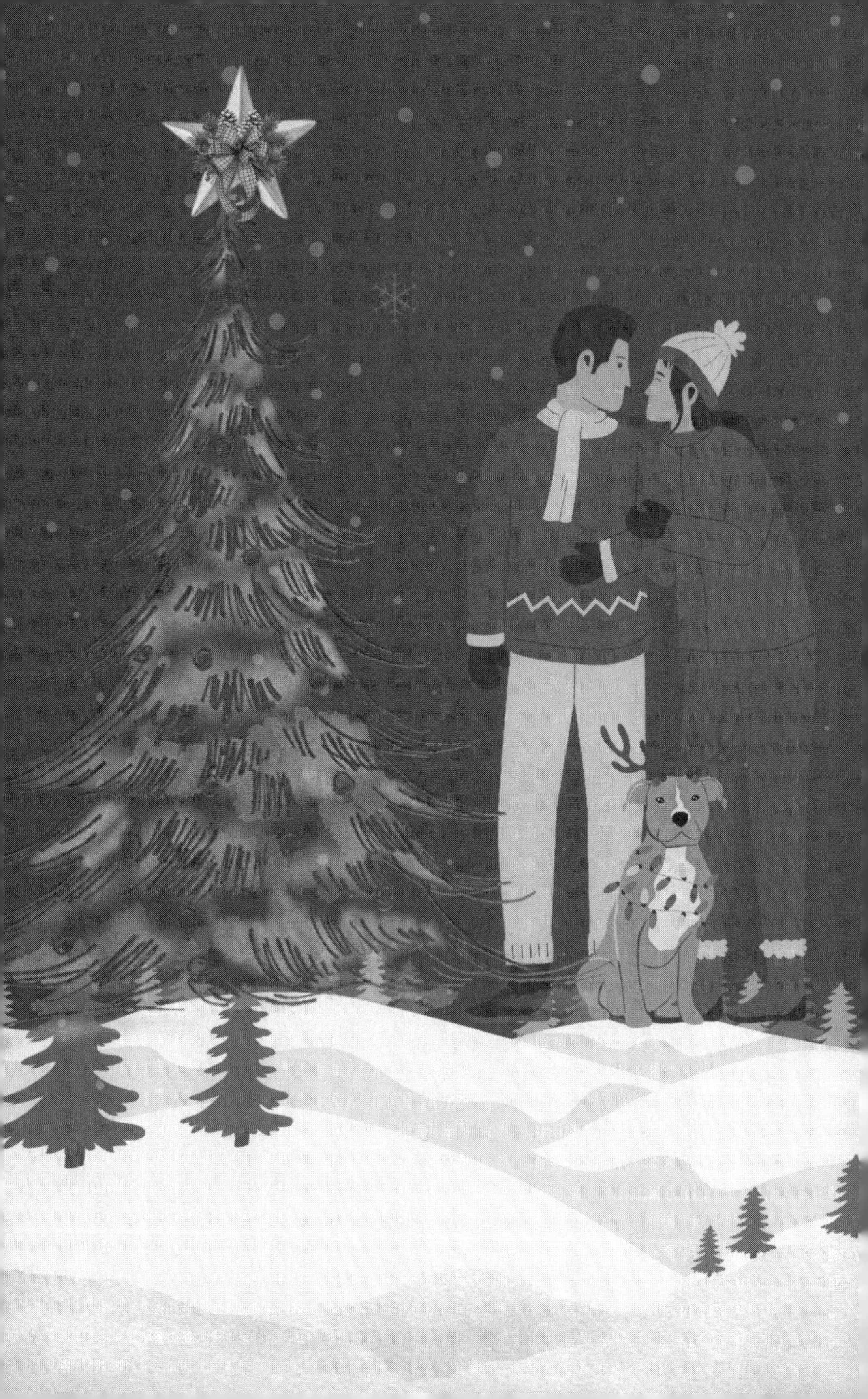

Chapter Four
Kash

I'm quite proud of myself for defending Stella where Gerry is concerned. I should've been an actor, pulling off empathy and the whole knight in shining armor routine at the same time. My indie performance of the year would've won an Oscar if there had been anyone around to film it. Mentally patting myself on the back for my outstanding job, I smile at how great it is to be a winner.

I focus on the dark-haired beauty next to me, but judging by her tight facial expression, she's still pissed off about the incident earlier this morning. She needs more cock in her life. There's no way a woman who is getting dicked like she deserves can be as unhappy and nervous as she is.

"So, you really don't care for vomit, huh?" I want to palm my forehead as soon as the words leave my mouth.

A glare that puts all others to shame, pulls at the features on her face. Shit, she really doesn't like puke. She turns to look out the passenger window, as if avoiding eye contact, when she answers. "I have an extremely weak stomach."

"I don't, so we'll make a good team. We can't have both of us barfing all over the place." I laugh, thoroughly enjoying the joke.

Catching her cringe out of the corner of my eye, I make the decision to choose my words more carefully to avoid more incidents involving stinky bodily fluids ending up on my dick. The rest of the ride from the hotel to the Mistletoe Creek Cafe is quiet and tense. I'm more than relieved when I park the car in front of the restaurant.

I chance a look at her. "Here we are. Let's order fried chicken and all the helpings, then we can talk."

"Mr. Saint, why are we here?" She purses her lips.

"We're redoing your job interview. I want to make sure it's a good fit for both of us." I sound professional enough and hope she'll just follow along with the plan, so I can fill my growling belly. I'm much less likely to be mercurial with higher blood sugar.

I don't give her the opportunity to ask more questions, which will only delay in ridding myself of the small hangover I'm carrying around. A large helping of grease and soul food will go a long way in appeasing my stomach and headache, although, I may need a nap after being rolled out of the diner.

Stella doesn't immediately move from the car, so I wait by the trunk and hope like hell she won't jump behind the wheel and back over me. I don't wait well. I'm impatient on a good day. Today is not a good day. Matty quit, and I've already run off the replacement. The hangover doesn't help matters either.

Bordering on losing my patience, I plaster on a smile and walk around to open her door. "You have to go *inside* to eat. That's how this works."

Her stomach growls on cue. "I'm not hungry, and I've already endured one job interview with you. I'm not doing another one."

"You're living in a seedy motel. I think you can afford to do another interview. It can only improve your chances at securing the job. As I'm sure you're aware, I'll make the final decision on hiring my assistant and paralegal." The truth is that I've never met anyone more qualified to be both, but I'm not letting her know that.

She considers my plea, narrowing her eyes as she thinks. "Fine. Will you leave me alone if I let you feed me?"

Visions of feeding her sweet, black grapes flitters through my mind and gives rise to the creature in my pants. "Yes." I settle with a one-word lie. I can't seem to manufacture more in her presence at the moment that aren't purely sexual in nature. I proffer my hand, which she eyes with an intense expression, before finally placing her small hand in my larger one.

We walk in complete silence to the front of the cafe, which I've been coming to since I moved to the town as a boy. I behave like a gentleman when we approach the door, opening it and waving her through as it chimes above. "Ladies first."

She pauses mid step, casts her big green eyes in my direction, and hesitates before sweeping the parking lot. "Thank you," she says so softly I almost miss it.

Just inside the door, Stella pauses. Focusing on her ass for a brief moment, I chide my dick to calm the fuck down. I find Stella intently studying each table for a few seconds. Then, she moves on to the next one. She reminds me of someone, but I can't put my finger on who.

The diner is only half full of patrons, but she seems ... nervous. "Is there a table you prefer?"

Her intense expression levels me. "Yes."

Holding my hand out toward the booths, I let her take the lead. "Please."

She points to the tables in the opposite direction, nestled along floor-to-ceiling windows. "Actually, I'd prefer the corner table next to the big window."

"I'm easy enough. I don't care where I sit, as long as I eat soon," I say as my stomach growls loudly enough for the entire cafe to hear.

At least, Stella hears. Her eyes lower to my belly and remain there for a long beat. "There's something living in your stomach."

I don't know why I find her response so funny, but a smile stretches across my face. "Yes, indeed. Pick a table and a seat so I can feed it."

She turns on her heel and moves in the direction of the corner table, taking the seat facing the front door. Casting several glances in the direction of the entrance, she finally lands on my face again. When she realizes I've noticed, she turns to the napkin dispenser and plucks two menus from behind it. "We might need these."

"I don't. I've eaten the same exact thing here for over a decade." I've been doing mainly the same shit for a decade all around.

Her gaze moves from one side of the laminated red menu to the other. "You never change it up?"

"No. I know what I like and what I want in virtually any situation. I'm not fixing something that isn't broken." When I hear the crap coming out of my mouth, it reminds me of my old man, and I'm not exactly sure how I feel about it.

"Variety is the spice of life, yeah?" she asks, and my mind goes straight to the gutter, but I read her sarcasm loud and clear.

Steepling my hands together and placing my elbows on the table, I do my best to move past our issues from this morning. "Can we start over?" I don't wait for her to reply, extending my hand across the table. "Hey, I'm Kash. I'm a local attorney who inherited his father's business. My long-time assistant quit this morning, and the truth is I need help preparing for a case I have next week. You have quite the background in contractual law, and I could use fresh eyes on it. I'll match Matilda's pay and benefits, starting immediately."

She eyes my hand, like it might contain the Ebola virus. After hesitating for a small eternity, she puts her dainty hand in mine. "Stella Black. I'm quiet and don't like to cause any trouble. I do have experience with contractual law in California and Georgia —"

I interrupt her as my ADHD brain jumps into gear. "How did you end up in Mistletoe?"

Her eyes dart to the side as she drops my hand. The discomfort in her body language rubs me the wrong way. I don't know her from Eve. She could be clinically insane ... or an axe-murderer. I watch the Discovery Channel and have been a practicing attorney long enough to know a pretty face isn't always what it seems.

"Are you on the run from law enforcement?" All I need is a fugitive working for me and causing me trouble.

Stella pulls her hands from the tabletop and hides them under the table.

I don't have time to investigate further when Dina interrupts the tension at our table. "Hey there, Kash. Is this your new assistant? Matilda was in here last night, telling everyone today was her last day. I can't believe she finally retired. The woman has to be seventy-five, if not a day." Dina turns to Stella. "Ain't you pretty as a peach? Lord have mercy, the eligible bachelors in Mistletoe are going to be fighting over the spots on your dance card, suga."

Two things occur to me — Stella is the prettiest woman in this town, or hell, maybe even the entire state of Tennessee. Most importantly, I realize that Dina is dead-on with how the men in this little place will react to her presence in town. It might not be a bad thing for her dance card to fill up a few nights a week. I've never met someone in more need of sex.

"Dina, please meet Stella Black. She's interviewing for the position at the firm. I owe her a meal for her time. How about if we start with coffee?" I don't bother asking if Stella drinks it. All legal professionals drink java. It's part of the reasons we can pull long days in court and even longer nights in the office.

"Coming right up!" Dina bounces away from the table, her dirty blonde ponytail swinging back and forth.

Refocusing my full attention on Stella, I hesitate to continue our conversation about her dodgy reaction.

"I'm not on the run from any legal entities." Her gaze moves back to my ear, very obviously ignoring my eyes.

There's an oddness in her response that I can't quite put my finger on, but the lawyer in me goes into overdrive as my next question rolls off my tongue without much thought. "Who *are* you on the run from?"

I'm not prepared for her next move, which is leaping from the booth and swiftly walking toward the entrance.

That escalated quickly.

I pull at the ends of my hair in frustration. Without Matty, I don't have a lot of time to prepare for the case I'm arguing next week. I can't do it without a good paralegal possessing expertise in contract law. Why do women have to be so fucking dramatic? Attempting to talk myself out of the bullshit obviously associated with her, I weigh my options. Without time or help, I'm quite frankly up Shit's Creek.

Stella has already reached the front door, opened it, and stepped through when I finally get my ass in gear and go after her. Casting a look in Dina's direction, I hold up a finger to indicate for her to hold our table. My long legs catch me up to her quickly, and just as she's opening the driver's door to her old car, I close it.

She spins around, looking like a scared, wounded animal ready to strike out to protect itself. "You're standing too close." It's a command for me to back the fuck up.

I heed her warning, not because I'm physically afraid of her, but because I remember being the kid who looked at my foster dad that way. It was before I realized he wouldn't harm me like all the others before him had. That man eventually became my adoptive father. It took a lot of patience on his part and a fair amount of time before I ever trusted he wouldn't beat me or worse.

Holding my hands up, I surrender to her and back up a step. The last thing I need is her clocking me in the face. I'm too pretty for a bloodied and bruised face.

Fresh tears spring into her green eyes, turning them into a shade of light sage, but they never spill over her lids. I watch her struggle with her emotions but have no idea what words of comfort she needs to feel better. Swallowing hard, I look away. Crying women are hard for any man to handle. It makes us feel helpless, which is not a state in which many of us are comfortable with.

Her stomach growls so loudly, I'm afraid it might have eaten itself. Her hand flies to her belly as if to cover the sounds already escaping it. I need to feed her, and not because of the growl, but because a pained expression crossed her delicate features when it did.

Without looking her in the face again, I completely ignore her tears and forge forward. "I'm going inside and ordering take-out for us both. If you're here when I get back, you'll have lunch. If not, I'll eat it myself. No skin off my back."

I don't give her a second to volley back a reply, turning on my heel and heading back inside to finish my order. I doubt she'll be here when I return.

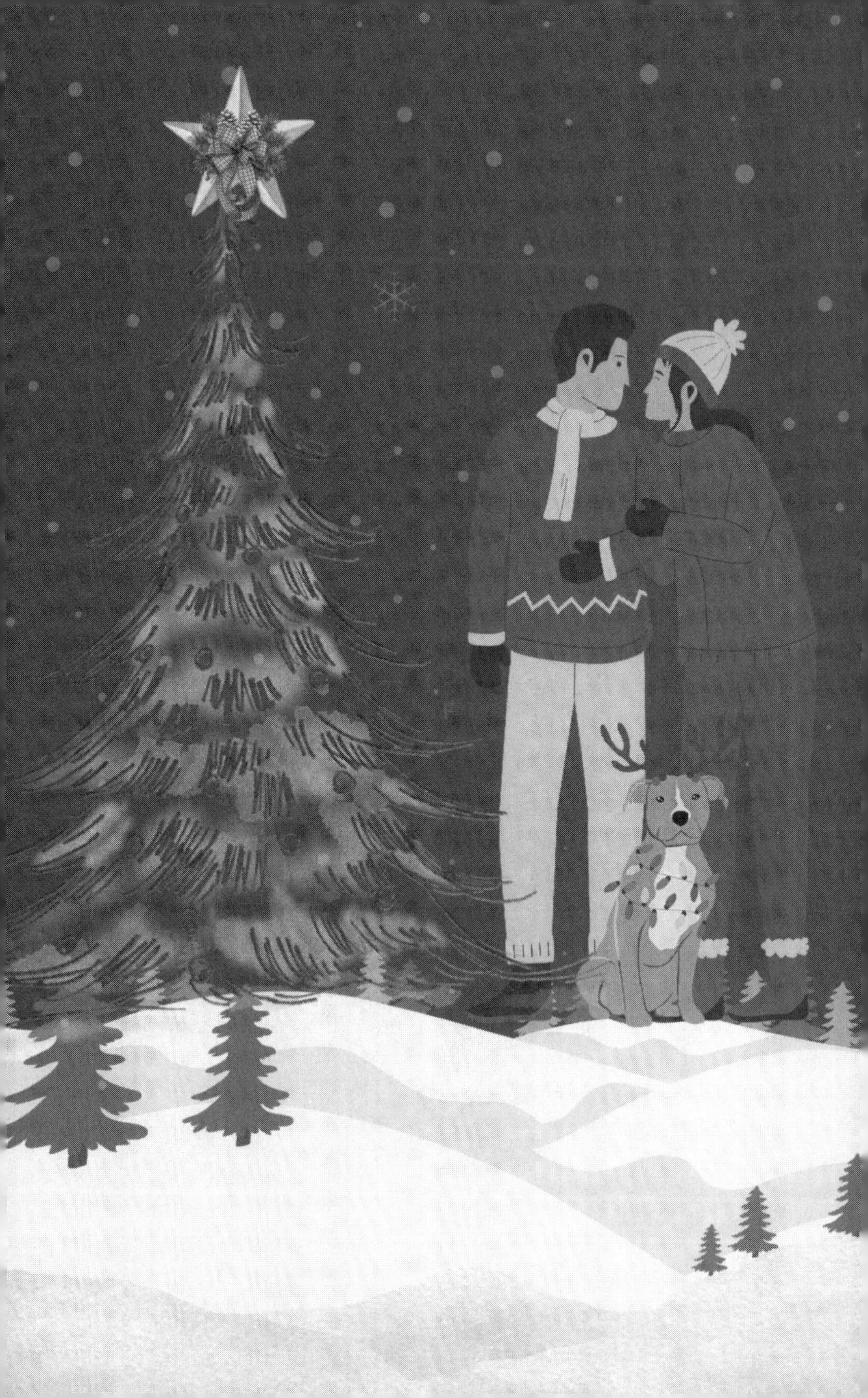

Chapter Five

Stella

My lip has grown sore from worrying it to death over the past few weeks. Being on the road alone while on the run from a psychopathic ex-boyfriend has left me in a constant state of panic.

Watching Kash walk away from me fills me with relief. I'm glued to the same spot for a long moment before I dive inside my car, close the door, and lock it. Without much thought, I turn the engine over and throw it in reverse. I need to get the hell out of here before my past catches up with me.

Pressing the brake, I shift the car into drive and turn the wheel. Before I can ease off the pedal and move to the accelerator, a loud thud comes from the back of my car. The hair on the back of my neck stands up when I realize I've hit a person.

Fuck!

My heart pounds in my ears, my chest grows tight, and my brain short circuits over what the hell I'm supposed to do now. Darren will surely get word of this when a police report is made for running over a person.

A loud, abrupt knock sounds at my window. I scream in response as my hand flies to my chest. "Ahhh!"

It takes a moment for the fear to clear my brain enough to recognize the man holding himself up with the help of my car — *Kash*. It's just my luck that I hit a freaking attorney, who's probably going to sue the shit out of me.

Attempting to open my door to help him, I do more damage by pushing him to the ground. I beat my fists on the steering wheel. "Grrrr. This is turning out to be a shittastic day."

I sigh and leave the vehicle, rushing to Kash's aid.

He's quick to hold up his big hand. "I'm okay. I just got the wind knocked out of me."

"I hit you!" I shriek at him, like he's not completely aware of the fact.

Without a second thought, I search his scalp for blood or visible damage. Head wounds are scary, but there's nothing to find in his short, dark hair. Pressing my hands to his shoulders, I look for wounds.

"What are you doing? Why are you touching me?" His annoyance is clear as day.

"Making sure I didn't hurt you." My rapid breaths are evident in my voice.

He waves off the notion. "I'm fine. Here." He pulls both of my hands into his and lifts them from my inspection beneath his ribs. "I'm okay. No harm, no foul. Okay?"

Examining his face, I attempt to determine if he's in a condition to make that call. *I hit him with a car.* Surely, he didn't escape unscathed.

Kash drops my hands and lifts his to my face, pulling me closer. "Breathe, Stella."

Suddenly realizing how close we are to each other makes it near impossible to catch my breath. "Um ..." I manage as I swallow hard.

His blue gaze lowers to my lips, and like an idiot, I do the same, awkwardly gawking at how delicious his red lips appear. I'm surprised when he clears his throat and looks away first.

What's wrong with me?

The awkward moment passes when he asks, "Can you help me up?"

Never one to turn down a change of subject, I rise and offer him my hand. He doesn't put much weight on my small arm as he follows me. He dusts off his expensive dress pants. The guilt over hitting him subsides as he moves toward my car. Two steps into his journey, he yelps out in pain. His leg bends at an odd angle, and he goes down again, falling to his ass and grunting in pain.

Uh-oh.

Kash clutches his leg and grimaces. Genuine pain falls across his masculine features.

I lower myself beside him, kneeling next to his injured leg. "I broke your leg."

"I highly doubt that little bump broke my leg." He scoffs as though a car, weighing tons, couldn't possibly damage him.

I'll chalk it up to a concussion or a direct result of the pain he's experiencing. Sighing, I search his suit jacket for a cell phone.

"Are you feeling me up while I'm injured and vulnerable?" He quirks a dark brow, his eyes sparkling with mischief.

"No, *Bunny*." I drop the not-so-subtle reminder that I stood in his kitchen this morning while three naked women were fresh off a weekend bender with him.

A deep bark of laughter leaves him. It's a genuine sound of happiness I find as sexy as I do comforting. If this guy can still find it in him to sincerely laugh at my jab, then maybe I have a real shot at making it without Darren there to control my every move.

"She has claws. I like you, Stella. Listen, would you be a doll and call me an ambulance? I'm feeling woozy." His dilated pupils concern me as his speech begins to slightly slur.

My anxiety ratchets up another ten notches. "Please don't die!"

Covering his ear, he frowns. "Got it. I'll do my best."

"Where's your phone?" My hurried words put my anxiety on full display.

I follow his opposite hand, reaching inside his jacket, and snatch it before he can grasp the device. The next few minutes are a haze of hyperventilating and a poor attempt at explaining the situation to the emergency services operator. After I disconnect the call, I glance down at the cell and try to remember what the heck I told the woman.

Hailing from larger cities, I'm not accustomed to the rapid response time of three different emergency providers in a small town like Mistletoe Creek. It almost seems like an ambulance, fire truck, and three law enforcement vehicles appear out of thin air in no time at all.

They swarm us, circling Kash, and asking him a myriad of questions about how his leg was injured. I freeze, not knowing what to do. Half the diner spills out into the parking lot, and all the locals gawk at me. Feeling on display, the urge to slowly back away, slide inside my car, and get the hell out of dodge almost takes over.

"She hit him! I saw her." A man, graying, with enough wrinkles to make a bulldog jealous, and beady eyes, points his finger at me.

On the verge of a panic attack, I begin to hyperventilate again, but Kash squeezes my hand.

"I stepped in that pothole over there, Jed," he says, crooking his finger over his shoulder to indicate the area behind us. "Y'all be careful back there."

The entire town turns to look for the pothole. Expecting everyone to call him out on his dishonesty, I'm shocked when they all nod like the hole suddenly filled itself.

"We'll get that filled for Dina." A dark-haired sheriff's deputy with whiskey brown eyes snaps his fingers and several of the townspeople move to fix the fictional hole. He turns his attention back to us, his gaze wandering over me. "Are you okay, ma'am? You're as white as a ghost." Again, he snaps his fingers, signaling to a few paramedics that I'm in distress.

I look like an idiot. I'm not the injured one. Meeting Kash's eyes with a plea for help, I find his face filled with pain. Guilt washes over me again, so I take a few deep breaths and get my shit together. I'm the reason he's in pain at all.

"Can we focus on Kash? I'm sure his leg is broken. He should really be taken to an emergency room sooner rather than later." I don't lift my eyes from him as I remind the men and women in uniform that they're here to do a job.

It seems to be exactly what they need to jump into action. Kash is loaded onto a gurney, which makes him grimace and grunt, but I can tell he's trying his hardest not to show it. Why do men have to be so damn tough?

Once he's loaded into the back of the ambulance, I stand at the open doors of the vehicle and wait. I'm not sure what to do next. Should I go with him in the ambulance? Follow behind it? Be a horrible human and get out of town as fast as my car will take me?

Kash calls out my name, his deep voice reaching me through a flurry of activity and voices. When my gaze meets his, he begins to speak, but closes his mouth as the rear ambulance doors shut.

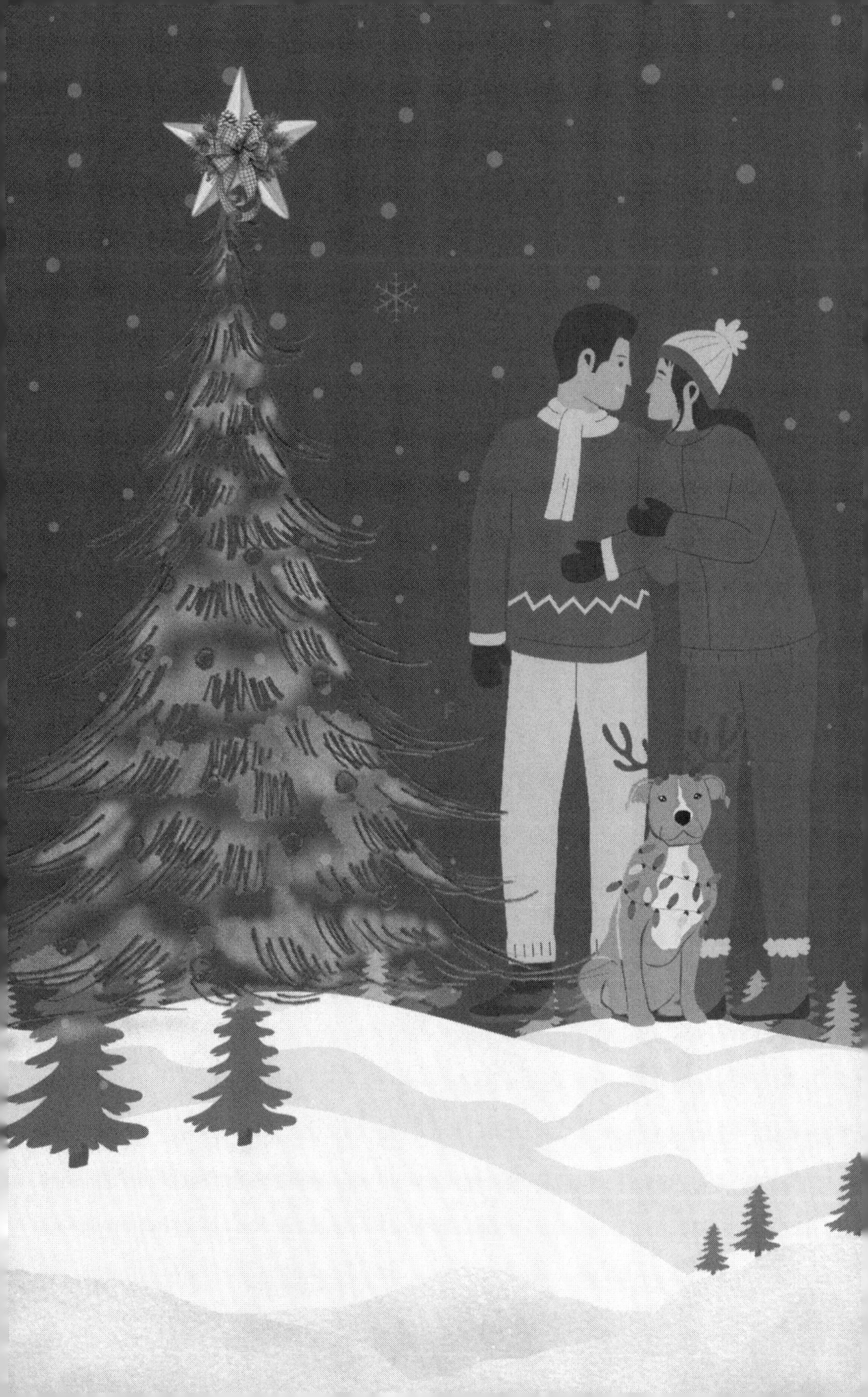

Chapter Six
Kash

We arrive at the emergency department in Mistletoe Creek Hospital, where I'm wheeled from the ambulance to a brightly lit room with one bed, two chairs, and a stool. I hope they'll give me good drugs to numb the throbbing pain in my leg.

The sliding glass door to my room moves to the side, and two seconds later, a gorgeous nurse in light blue scrubs steps past the curtain. Once I move past the high, blonde ponytail to her face, my heart drops.

"Well, if it isn't Kash Saint." The vaguely familiar woman's hands go to her curvy hips. "I heard a woman hit you with her car. Can't say it surprises me in the least. What did you do?"

Word travels fast in a small town.

"I stepped in a pothole …." I look over to a whiteboard on my right for help with her name. "… *Kerri.*"

Suddenly remembering her from the immediate period after my father died, I cringe. I probably didn't leave the best impression with her either.

"Hmph." She nears the bed, placing her hand on my aching leg. "I'm surprised you remember my name."

"What are you doing?" I sit up straight in case I need to fight her off.

She squeezes my leg just enough to make me wish I still had coke running through my veins. A pained grunt leaves me before I can stop it.

"Can you rate your pain, if zero is none and ten is the worst pain you've ever felt?" Kerri smirks at me.

Great. I pissed off a sociopath.

"*Excuse me.* Tell me I *did not* just see you do what you just did to a patient," a sweet voice comes from the entrance, but there's menace in her words.

My heart can't decide if it wants to turn somersaults or kick me in the ribs, so it does both. Looking around Kerri, I land on the dark-haired beauty I never thought I'd see again.

Stella.

A man with brown hair slicked back on either side of his part and dull brown eyes steps inside the room. His white coat leads me to believe he's a physician. "Hi, Mr. Saint, I'm Dr. Dawson. Can you tell me what happened?"

After a brief explanation of the pothole lie, I explain the type of pain I'm having and how much it hurts. Stella and Kerri end up in a staring standoff, and my attention goes straight to the cat fight that I semi-wish would break out. My money is on Stella. I miss whatever the doc is jabbering about.

Dr. Dawson's oblivious ass finally notices there might be a serious problem between these two. "What's going on, Kerri?

Kerri directs her saccharine smile at him. "I'm not sure?"

Stella's pouty mouth opens to speak, but I cut her off before she can cause damage to Kerri's career. I probably deserve the squeeze for whatever I did to her. "Kerri is an old friend of mine, and Stella is the new girlfriend." I lean toward the doctor, whispering to him. "Her jealousy's hot, isn't it?"

Stella and Kerri scoff at the same time, prompting me to chuckle nervously as I launch a prayer into the universe that Stella doesn't rat me out on the girlfriend lie.

"They hate when you point it out," I continue lying through my teeth.

Dr. Dawson's gaze cycles between the three of us - confused and unsure of how to proceed. "Kerri, would you mind sending in another nurse, please?"

Kerri's gaze lands on me, and I swear on everything sacred in this world, the woman's eyes glow with barely contained anger. I remind myself to run in the other direction if I ever come across her in public. She leaves the room without any further incident, which allows Stella to visibly relax.

The doc speeds through an explanation of the next steps, consisting of an x-ray, bloodwork, and pain meds. When he exits my room, Stella moves across it to the two chairs on my right, taking a seat in one and crossing one leg over the other.

I don't have another chance to speak with her about anything before a new nurse with short, chestnut brown hair and crystal blue eyes slides into the room to stick me with an IV, draw blood, and push pain meds. Within seconds of the morphine hitting my system, a warm and blissfully fuzzy state washes over my entire body, and not long after, another woman wheels me to another area for an x-ray.

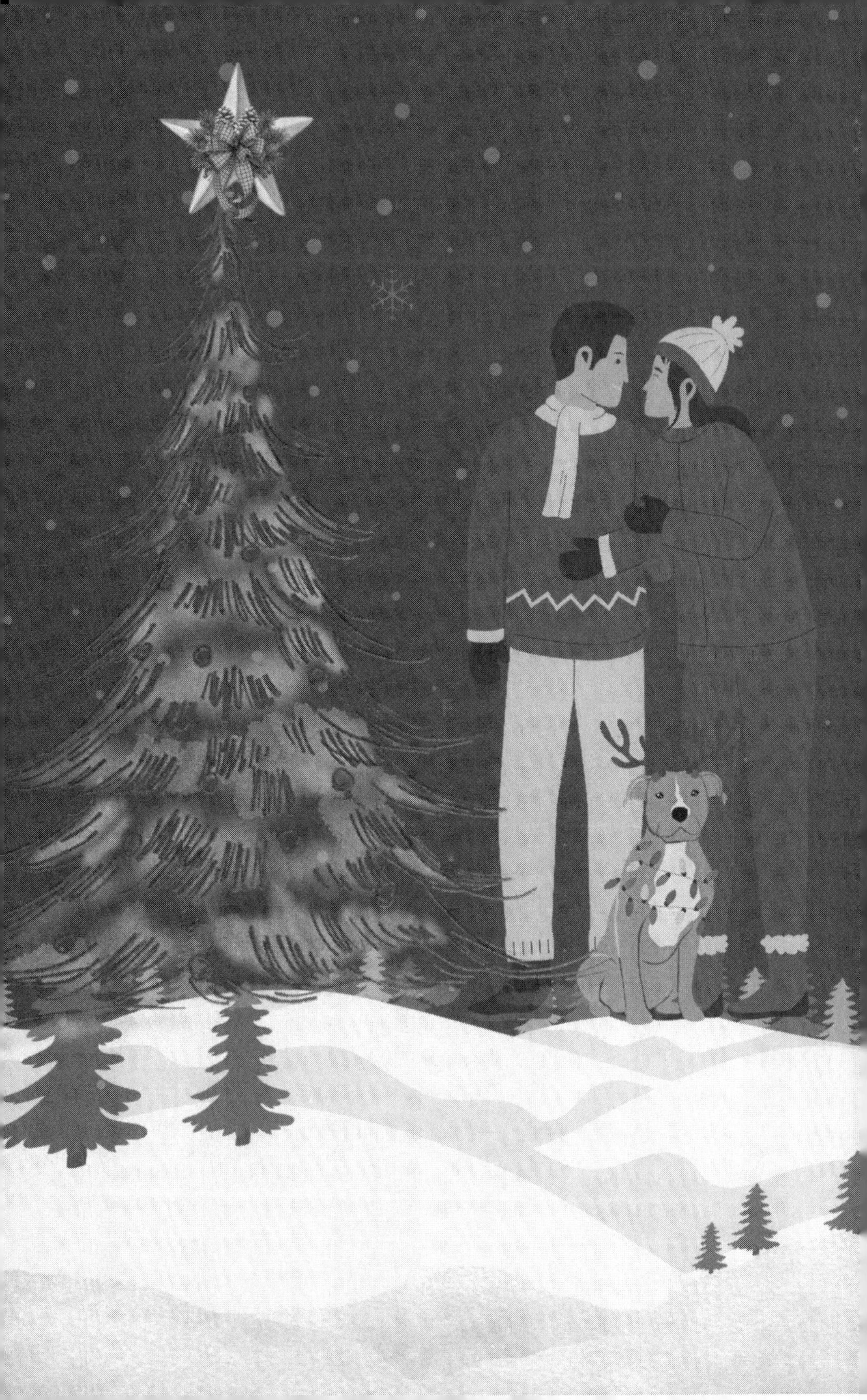

Chapter Seven
Stella

I sit alone in Kash's hospital room, debating whether to stick around for news on his injured leg. The smart thing to do would be to get the hell out of here before someone runs my name through the system. Fidgeting with my hands, my conscience reminds me I'm not a bad person for wanting to escape Darren. I deserve to be free of abuse and toxic behaviors, just like all the women I helped accomplish just that before I gained the courage to leave Darren and find it for myself.

After enduring two years of misery with him, I woke up one day several weeks ago and began making a plan to leave everything behind. I quit my job as a paralegal in Atlanta, cashed out a small retirement, and bought everything I could to prepare for this new journey. The night before I left, he served with me the last black eye I swore he'd ever give me. I snuck out in the middle of the night with a used car parked around the corner, full of clothes, toiletries, water, and meal-ready food.

Driving all over the southeast for a few weeks, I landed in Mistletoe Creek, Tennessee, where I parked in the Mistletoe Creek Café for a few hours and watched the locals flock to the good food inside. It's Christmas time, so I attributed the joy seemingly emanating from the townspeople to the season.

My car needed gas, so I pulled it over to the nearest station and filled the tank. After visiting the facilities, I bought a local and national paper to check for Darren using law enforcement tactics to lure me out. I wouldn't put it past him to file a missing person report on me. Not finding the first thing about me in either paper was relieving, but I did run across an ad for a paralegal and legal assistant position at a nearby law firm. I needed money, as the meager amount I began my journey with was quickly dwindling to nothing.

I had to settle somewhere, and this was as good a place as any. Sending up a prayer, I returned to my car and emailed my resume from my phone to the address in the listing. Matilda phoned me back within half an hour. Hoping for both an advance and to be paid in cash to allow me to fly under the radar, I found a truck stop to park in overnight until I could be ready for the interview the next day.

Fast forward to the present, where I've hit a man, possibly broken his leg, and ruined any chances of an advance, a job, and a place to lie low.

Before I can make a decision to stay or go, Kash is wheeled back into the room, and fortunately, he's sound asleep. That's my cue to get out of here before it's too late.

Just as I reach the door, his groggy voice reaches my ears. "If you leave, it'll make it a hit and run."

Ticked off by the insinuation, I spin around. "I *did not* hit and run. I got out of my vehicle and called for help. If I remember correctly, I also made sure you were swiftly brought here, seeing as the town was more worried about fixing in your fictional pothole than your leg."

He doesn't even flinch at me calling out the lie. Kashton Saint looks me dead in the eye and defends his dishonesty. "I do recall that lie saving your ass."

"From what exactly? An accidental injury? I didn't hit you intentionally, and we both know it. As a matter of fact, what the heck were you doing behind my car while I was rolling backward? Did you walk into my car on purpose?" My hands fly to my hips, waiting for him to deliver another guilt trip for hitting him.

"You're on the run from someone or something. I didn't think you'd want any attention brought to you, so I took responsibility for the accident. A lie told to help someone isn't really a lie at all."

My brows almost touch my hairline. "That's not always true. Sometimes people are dishonest to help bad people."

He doesn't miss a beat. "Are you a bad person?"

Averting my gaze to the floor, I have to consider his question before I answer. I preached to other women for years about the importance of getting away from their tormentors and protecting their children in the process. Meanwhile, Darren was leaving bruises from the sixth month of our relationship forward, but I smiled when those women looked at pictures of him and I in my office and told me how lucky I was to have a good man. That makes me a hypocrite. "I don't know."

"That's hardly true—" Kash cuts his sentence short when the short brunette nurse from earlier returns to the room.

After briefly checking his pain, she promises to return when the x-ray is read by the radiologist.

Once she's gone, Kash changes the subject. "Look, you're hungry, exhausted, and you've had a rough day. Let's save these arguments for our next interview."

"What interview?" I ask, thoroughly confused by his statement.

"The one we're having as soon as this leg is set and the morphine wears off —"Kash stops short when Dr. Dawson steps back into the room.

After hanging an x-ray film on a light box, the doctor explains Kash's leg is indeed broken, but can be set without surgery. I breathe out a small sigh of relief. At least, I won't have to pay for thousands of dollars of surgical bills. The ambulance ride and the emergency room fees will set me back a long time as it is.

Kash asks for more pain medication before they set the bone and wrap his leg in a cast. I can't say I blame him for asking for I.V. courage. I'm grateful for it myself, especially when I hear his muffled yelp of pain from outside his hospital room. Guilt seeps into my bones, no matter how hard I try to tell myself that I didn't harm him on purpose. My empathy bone is huge.

His nurse invites me back inside his room once the cast is in place. Worrying my bottom lip, I head back inside with my shoulders slumped and defeat sinking in. Maybe Darren was right when he said I couldn't make it without him.

"Why are you sulking? I'm the one in pain," Kash barks at me from his bed.

I forgive him because he's in immense pain, but I do manage a small jab. "You have drugs."

His expression turns sheepish as if he might actually be ashamed about being rude to me. "They're going to discharge me with a script for meds here shortly. It would be nice if you could get those filled and help me find my way home and into my bed."

"You have a case to prepare for," I remind him. I've never taken a day off work, because I've never had the luxury. Life wasn't as kind to me as it was to Kash where his adoption is concerned. I've also never been fortunate enough to call out of a job because of an injury. I picked myself up and brushed myself off.

Life fucking hurts.

But I suppose I owe him as much as filling his prescription and seeing him home. Whether it was intentional or not, I'm responsible for injuring him.

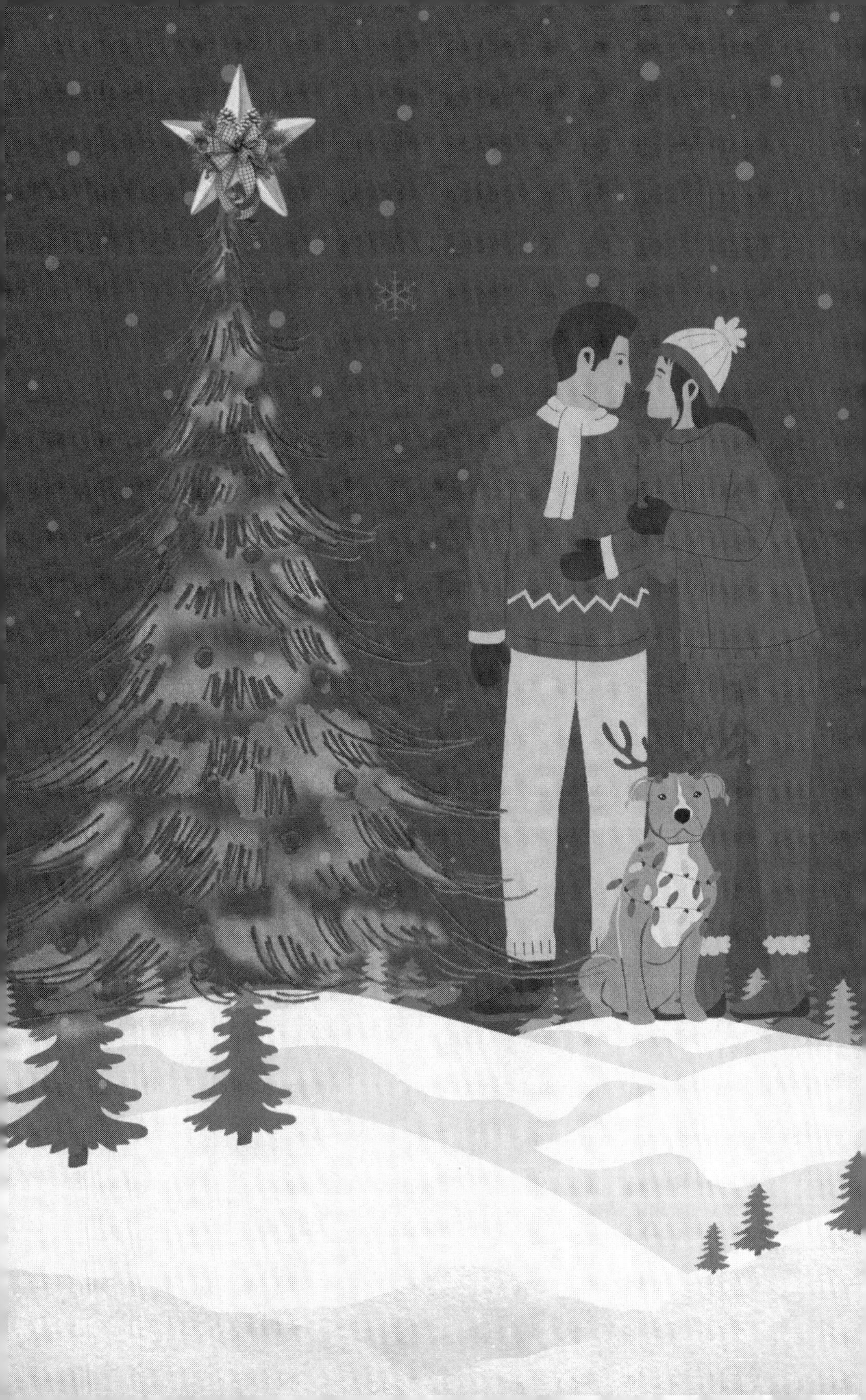

Chapter Eight

Kash

"H ey."

A hard shove at my shoulder startles me awake. Opening my eyes, I open my heavy lids, finding more than one, blurry Stella staring back at me. I attempt to speak, but my tongue is so dry, it sticks to the roof of my mouth.

Stella cringes at my froggy, garbled words. "That sounded painful."

My parched throat makes my second try at speaking impossible. I finally push a whisper from my diaphragm. "Water."

"Here." She steps to the right before returning with a glass of water in her hand.

Whatever the nurse pushed into my I.V. at discharge time must've been an extra dose. "When did we come home?" I ask, lazily gazing around my bedroom.

Accepting the drink from her, I chug it down as soon as it touches my lips.

"Around midnight. You were a great deal of help getting your big self into the house and bed." Her annoyed sarcasm is loud and clear.

"You stayed." I'm not sure why it surprises me — her staying the night when she could've simply dropped me off at the front door to fend for myself.

Her green eyes dart to the side as discomfort slides across her shoulders. "I need to make sure you aren't going to cause any problems for me when I leave."

Again, she reminds me of someone, but my brain is on really good drugs, so I can't put my finger on who it is. "How would I cause you problems?"

She worries her bottom lip but brings her attention back to me. "If you report me for a hit and run, it will likely reach the wrong person. Then he'll come after me."

"He." I'm glad she verified the tidbit of information about whomever she's running from.

Throwing the dark gray comforter off me, I move toward the edge of my bed, completely forgetting about my broken leg. I grunt in pain as a slew of profanities pour from my mouth. "Fuck! That hurts like a bitch!"

"Slowly." Stella's voice is gentle.

It tugs at a memory from my early formative years, but my brain is full of fuzz. I can't seem to make the connection.

"Are you okay?" She's worried.

The concern pulls my gaze back to her, but the words stick in my throat.

Stella reaches out to touch my shoulder. "You look like you've seen a ghost."

Clearing my throat, I move away from her uncanny comment. "Mind helping me sit up and move to the edge of the bed?"

"Of course." She moves a hair closer and offers her hand.

My large hand slides across hers, being careful not to apply too much pressure on her small, delicate frame. We work well together in getting me to the side of my bed. It takes me several seconds to gain my bearings. "How long have I been asleep?"

Glancing at the clock on my nightstand, she takes a moment to answer, computing her answer. "If you count sleeping at the hospital, you've been asleep for eighteen hours."

"What the fuck did they give me at the hospital? Horse tranquilizers?" I joke.

Disappointment settles across her features. "No, you're exhausted from your busy weekend. Pain can also fatigue a person. They pushed too much morphine." She says the last part more to herself.

Briefly thinking Kerri may have had a friend try to off me, I make a note to myself not to screw anymore nurses or doctors. They're the last people I need holding a grudge.

"Have you ever used crutches?" She steps over to a pair, leaning against the wall closest to my bed.

"No, but thanks to you, I'll now have the pleasure." My remark sparks her frown.

"Why did you stand behind a car moving in reverse?" She snarks.

"I thought you saw me." I growl at her. I'm not in the mood to put up with her misplacing the blame.

"Cool. Well, you have fun with these then." She releases the crutches and allows them to fall to the floor.

"What's that mean?" I don't appreciate the attitude being thrown in my direction.

Turning on her heel, Stella gives me her back side and walks toward the door.

"Hey! Where the fuck are you going?!" The shout causes a sharp pain to tear through my throat.

When she reaches the door, she looks over her shoulder and lifts one middle finger into the air.

Once she disappears from my room for longer than I'm comfortable with, I yell after her. "Hey! You owe me!"

My front door slams a second later. Part of me hopes I never see her face again. She's been a drama Queen and suspicious as fuck from the word go. But as I look down at the crutches, a much smaller part of me wishes I had the sense to learn how to use the damn things before I pissed her off. Hindsight is a bitch sometimes.

Well, to hell with Stella. I can do this on my own. Reaching down, I lean as far as I can, extending my arm as far as it'll go, but they're still not within my grasp. I scoot down the bed and put myself closer. I've got this. It only takes one more try to pull the first one into my hand. The second half of the set is just as easy to secure.

While it would be nice to have Stella around to help with the Rutgers case, I'm thankful for dodging the bullet.

I take a deep breath and hoist myself onto the crutches, but they're not for a man of my height. Actually, I'm pretty sure they're for a child. I lose my balance, wobble on my good leg, and fall backward toward the bed. I miss it, my back hitting the side, and I slide down to the floor with a hard thud, which only serves to make the throb in my leg more severe.

I make several attempts at pulling myself up from the floor but quickly wear myself out. The gym is calling my name. I'm closer to forty than I am thirty, and the women won't sleep with an out-of-shape dude. I can't just be a pretty face. I need to be the entire package.

Wishing like hell that Stella would come back and help me off the fucking floor, I work on catching my breath before I move toward my nightstand. Here's to hoping my cell phone is there.

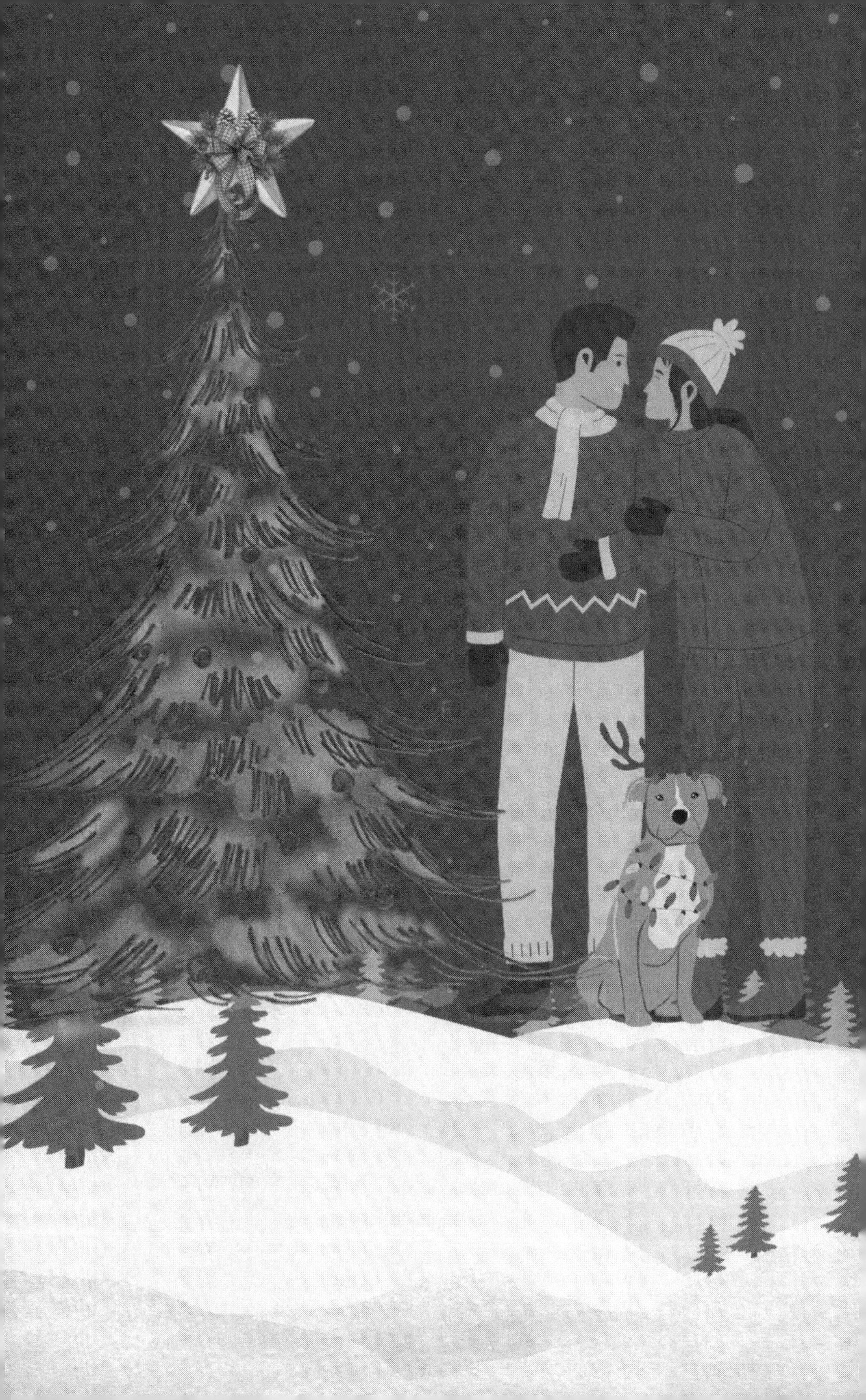

Chapter Nine
Stella

Sitting in Kash's driveway, I war with my crippling anxiety. If he becomes vindictive over me leaving him alone, he could cause me a world of trouble, and it's trouble I frankly don't need again.

Mistletoe Creek might be the worst decision I've made since leaving Darren a few weeks ago, and meeting Kashton Saint is 1000% the worst thing to happen since my escape. He's an insufferable ass when he's not injured. I can't imagine the extremes in which he's going to play the sympathy card on the townspeople.

My conscience shouts at me to run away from him and this place. At this rate, I might as well leave the state of Tennessee too, just to be safe.

Sirens wail in the distance. The hair on the back of my necks stands up, fear spiking my heart rate and blood pressure.

He called the cops on me! The nerve of that asshole!

If I would've known he'd endanger my life for shits and giggles, I would've slammed my foot on the accelerator and ran completely over him, put the car in drive, and ran back over him to make sure I did the best job possible.

Finding myself an inch past pissed off, I kill my ignition, wrench my door open, and march into Kash's house. I can't say I don't experience joy when I discover him in the middle of the floor with the crutches splayed in two different directions.

He couldn't get up on his own, and it serves him right.

"Did you really call the cops on me?" I don't bother tampering the anger in my voice.

"I didn't call the cops on you," he growls between clenched teeth.

It dawns on me that the man didn't call them on me at all. He called them to help him off the floor. Guilt washes over me, since I'm the reason he's down there in the first place.

I'm a terrible person.

Sighing, I close the space between us, pick up the crutches, and move them closer to him. It's the only form of an apology he's ever going to receive from me.

I offer him my hand, hoping to give him the boost he needs. He yanks on me, catching me completely by surprise and knocking me off balance. I fall forward. My hand shoots out to prevent me from falling on him and injuring him further. I'm not sure why I'm so freaking concerned about him when he deserves whatever he gets after pulling me toward him.

My foot tangles with his long legs on my way down and pitches me forward, causing my ample chest to slam into his face at the same exact moment his front door bursts open. Kash's large hands fly to my hips, not to help me, but to remove me from his personal space. Dizziness overtakes me as I slide down the front of him and hit both knees.

Pain radiates from the middle of my legs in every direction. I shut my eyes to prevent tears from spilling over. Holy fuck, that hurt like hell.

When I open them, there's shock playing across Kash's features. He clears his throat, shifts underneath me, and alerts me to the presence of his hard pecker. My eyes widen of their own accord.

He looks down at my lips, quickly averting his attention just below them. "Don't move."

The command in his voice leads to the involuntary clenching of my thighs and vagina. A whisper of a moan leaves me. It takes me a few seconds to realize the sound came from me, which heats my cheeks with embarrassment.

At the most inopportune moment in my life, his bedroom fills with firemen, sheriff deputies, and paramedics. The room falls silent as I debate whether to expose Kash's erection and flee the scene. Either way, we look ... friendly ... too friendly.

A nervous masculine laugh fills the room. "Looks like you got the help you needed, buddy."

I glare at the crowd. "I tripped."

A nasally snort is followed by a round of snickers from the group.

"Uhhhhh, so you tripped and landed on his —"

Kash's deep voice booms in response. "Don't finish that sentence, dipshit. She literally tripped, and yes, fell in my lap as a result of her trying to avoid messing up my pretty face."

Just when I think he might possess a shred of decency, he reminds me to listen to intuition more often. It tells me Kashton Saint isn't a good man. He has no morals, in addition to being a self-centered asshole and a sex-crazed pervert.

I have this stupid condition where I try to find the best in people. Until Darren did a number on me, I, at one time, believed there was good in everyone. The man I'm straddling might not beat women or use his job to hurt people and protect his crimes, but he's a bad egg — rotten to the core.

Releasing a frustrated groan, I remove myself from this ridiculous situation, placing a hand on either of Kash's shoulders and pushing myself off his lap. I don't miss the twitch of the beast in his sleeping pants.

Kash fights against me, pulling me down to keep me in his lap. "I thought she'd left me," he tells the room as he continues to wrestle against my attempt to run away.

"Ah, a lover's quarrel," someone standing behind me says.

"What?! Hell n—" I begin, but he slides his big hand over my mouth.

"She loves me." There's a smile in Kash's voice as he lies to the entire room.

Growing weary of fighting against him, I slam my ass down on his lap, giving him exactly what he wants. Let's hide his erection.

The room collectively cringes. "Ouch."

A high-pitched squeak leaves him. "Assault." His words are strangled from pain.

The gang of first responders laugh loud enough to wake the dead, then they file out of the room while murmuring to each other about the chances we have at making it as a couple.

I shiver from repulsion at the mere suggestion. The front door closes before my hips are released by the idiot underneath me. Leaving this town is imperative at this point. There are now people who think I'm screwing King Ding-a-ling. There's not a chance in hell.

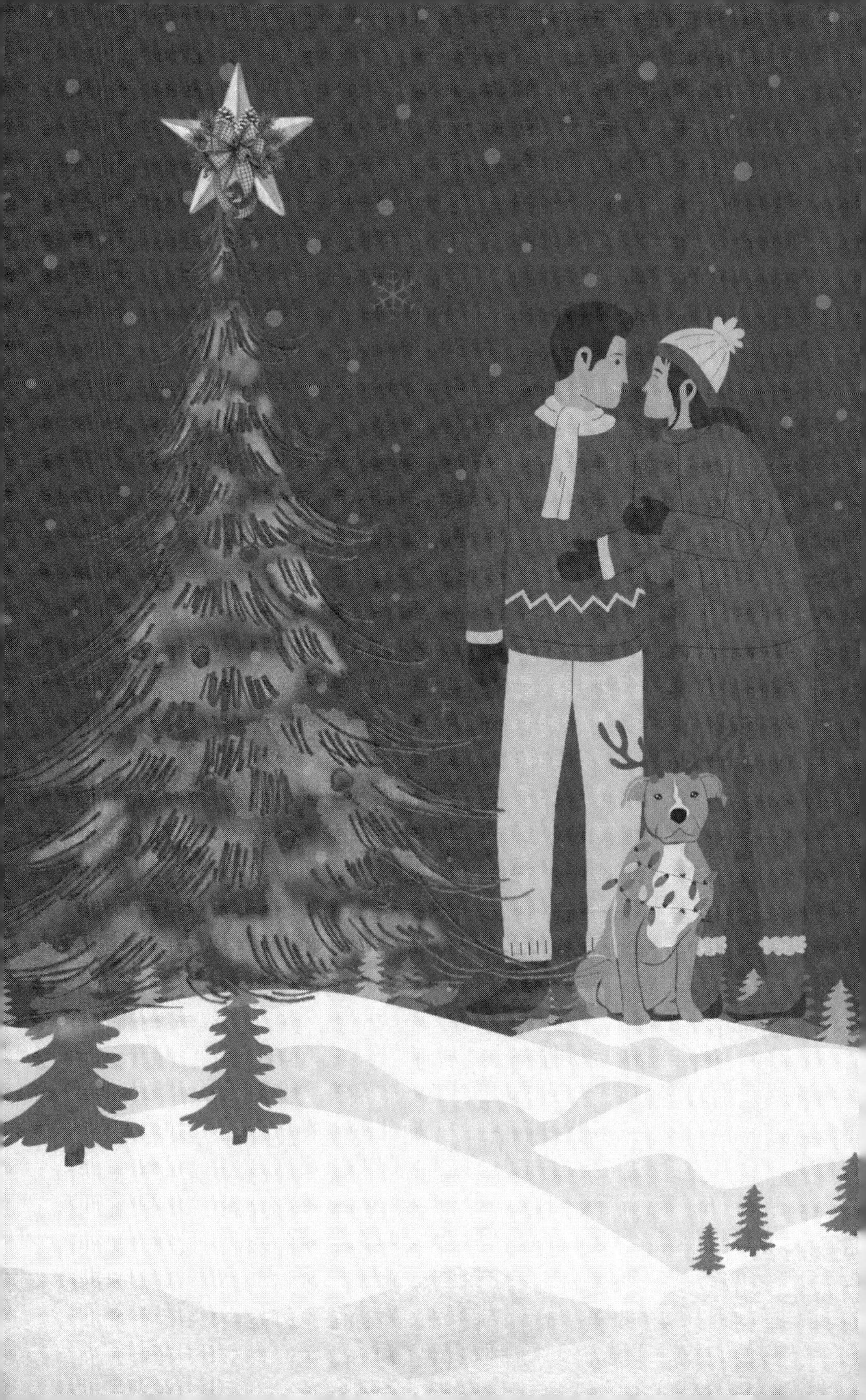

Chapter Ten
Kash

My dick wants to crawl inside my body. I resist the urge to curl into the fetal position and fight the nausea threatening to make an appearance.

"Ugh! You are the worst!" Stella pushes at my chest in frustration and quickly moves off my lap.

Grunting at the relief that follows, I fight another wave of nausea.

She rights her clothing from our brief entanglement, narrows her eyes in my direction, and huffs. "I hope you contract syphilis. If anyone deserves it, it's you."

"That's harsh. Why would you wish that on Jack?" I'm taken aback by her venomous tone and the malicious intent toward my favorite appendage.

She opens her pretty mouth, but stops short, holds up a finger, and shakes her head. "No. I'm not doing this with you. I hope your leg heals in record time. I wish you and Jack the best, but you're on your own."

I don't have a chance to object before she turns on her heel and hauls ass out of my room. Panic takes over when the front door slams against the jamb.

You're on your own.

I most certainly can't be left on my own. I'll fuck life up worse than I already have. My father is dead, Matilda is gone, and now, Stella has left too. My chest grows tight at the mere suggestion of being alone.

Alone.

I've been an orphan ... *twice.*

Shaking my head, I leave the clusterfuck of my mind and work up a sweat while trying to pull myself off the floor. The crutches are awkward to walk with, but I manage to make it across the house and to my front door swiftly. Peeking through sheer white window curtains, I have a look at the drive, discovering Stella pacing beside it.

She pulls at her long dark brown hair. Her mouth is moving, so she must be having a conversation with herself since there's no one else around to hear.

Before she decides to get into her car and leave, I fight with the door and two crutches, finally opening it and leaning against the frame. Slightly out of breath, I call out to her. "How's the convo going?"

She spins around to face me. "What convo?"

I shrug. "I suppose the one you're having with yourself?"

Stella rolls her green eyes, not bothering to hide her disenchantment with me. "You wouldn't understand, because I was arguing with my guilty conscience."

A frown tugs at my mouth. "What's that supposed to mean?"

She throws her hands up in irritation. "It means you don't have a conscience at all! You're self-centered, possess no scruples, and ... and!" She shakes a finger at me.

"And what?"

"You're a sex-crazed lunatic!" She yells across the yard for all of Mistletoe Creek to hear, not that the town isn't aware of my prowess.

Doing my level best to keep a straight face, I fail miserably at hiding the amusement in my voice. "*Sex-crazed lunatic?*"

Her hands fly to her hips, and she purses her pouty red lips. "I said what I said."

I don't know why I find her response to be cute, but it is. Stella doesn't appreciate the smirk on my face, if her groaning and wrenching open her car door is any indication.

An odd, foreign feeling washes over me – desperation – and before I can stop it the words fly out of my mouth. "Ten thousand dollars."

My impulsive tactic to stop her in her tracks works. Nobody sneezes at that much money, but especially not a woman on the run. Cash can help her greatly in hiding from the man she's so fearful of.

Stella turns her dark head, and her gaze sears me from over her shoulder, but she doesn't say anything.

"Ten thousand dollars for one case, and you'll have a safe, rent-free place to stay while we work. I'll even hide your car in the garage out back. If you don't want to stay after the case is over, I'll help you secure documents to start a new life." I sweeten the deal, because I need her help with these fucking crutches as much as I need her assistance with my next case.

I'm pleasantly surprised when she closes her door and heads in my direction. She climbs the stairs to the front porch and comes to a stop in front of me. She has to crane her neck back slightly to look at me. "I have stipulations if I'm to consider your offer."

It takes a valiant effort on my part not to sigh at the guidelines she's about to lay out for my behavior. She's not the first woman to do this, but this is the first time I don't have a choice but to stand here and agree to her rules. "I'm listening."

"You'll remain sober during working hours, which includes weekend business hours, if they're needed for the case. You'll not have any blonde, brunette, or auburn-flavored distractions while we're working on this case. You must be on time to work and ready to work each morning by 8 am. You'll need to dress and behave professionally at all times. I'll find other living arrangements until the case is over." She counts the stipulations on her hand, releasing a new finger with each new law she lays down.

"There's an apartment over the garage in the back. It needs some sprucing up but would be a good place for you to lay your head. There's not much for rent in this town." Hoping she'll take me at my word and stay, I maintain my poker face even though I'm not being completely honest.

"Do you agree to my stipulations?" she asks, quirking a brow in an attempt to cover her true interest in my offer.

I extend my hand to her. "Shake on it?"

Stella hesitates, biting her bottom lip and showing her nerves, but finally slides her palm across mine. "You are agreeing to no booze, drugs, or women."

"Is it so hard to believe a sex-crazed lunatic can refrain from temptation?" It takes a small miracle, but I hide the laughter threatening to boom from my belly at the insult.

She doesn't hold back. "Yes, but I'll give it a shot. If I had any other options, I wouldn't be standing here, but you already know that."

I shake her hand up and down, knocking myself off balance again and crashing to the porch. I don't miss the sigh leaving Stella.

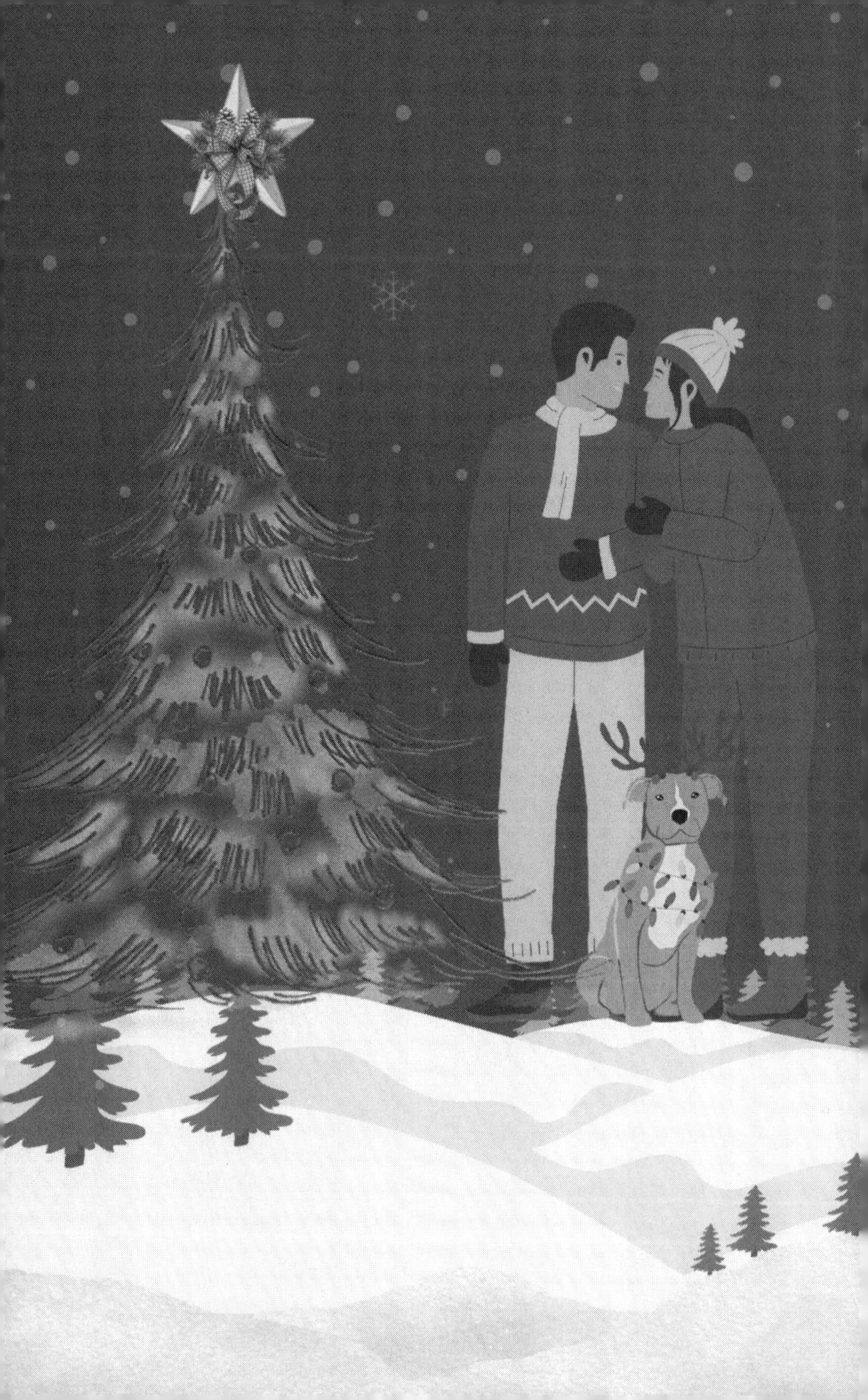

Chapter Eleven
Stella

Much to my surprise, Kash is waiting for me in the kitchen the next morning. Even more impressive is him holding out a travel mug filled with a creamy coffee concoction, which appears to meet my standards. Doubting his ability to not screw it up, I accept the drink and hesitantly take a sip.

It's yummy with the perfect amount of sugar and milk, but I withhold the moan it threatens to produce. When I lift my gaze to him, Kash is waiting for my reaction.

"Well? I killed it, didn't I?" He's more than proud of himself.

"How did you know how I like my coffee?" I'm more than suspicious of the intimate knowledge.

He lifts a shoulder. "It's how Matilda takes hers. Just a lucky guess."

"Thank you for the coffee and for being ready on time." I move us toward the vehicle, stepping into the cool December morning and enjoying the slight shiver that ripples through me.

There's nothing better than crisp, mountain air. It reminds me of a brief time in my childhood when I was safe under my grandfather's care. He didn't know anything about raising a child, but my mother was long gone by the time I entered grade school. My earliest memories of her are vague at best, but I remember her father. He was a kind man with long, white hair and matching beard, but he was old, and time always takes its toll.

After some maneuvering of his crutches, we make the short ride to the office where I initially interviewed with Matilda. It's a quiet trip, but not uncomfortably so. He seems to be as lost in his thoughts as I am in mine.

When we arrive at the Law Offices of Saint & Fox, a round, balding man and a tall, leggy blonde with bright red lips, are waiting on us. I barely register the historic home that houses their business because the man opens Kash's door before I can shift the vehicle into park.

He seems excited to see Kash, but I find it odd that the first time I'm seeing or hearing from his partner is well after the man should've stopped by to check on him. Meeting the blonde's stare, I lift a questioning brow, silently asking her what the hell her problem is. She mimics me by also quirking her brow, as if to challenge me.

I completely miss Fox helping Kash from my car, but thank Heavens, they emerge and intervene when they do. I'm growing more concerned by the second that she's going to turn to physical means of intimidation. She looks meaner than cat shit.

"Take a breather, Kitty," Kash's deep command booms from the other side of the car.

Who names a child "Kitty"?

The woman twists on her heel, whips her head around, and marches off in the opposite direction. The click-clack of her heels is all that follows. It's difficult to tell at this stage, but I'm positive she's not going to be my fan.

Leaving the topic of Kitty until we're alone, I walk with the two men in silence to the back of the yellow house.

Once we reach Matilda's desk, I get the formality over with. "Hi, I'm Stella, Matilda's temporary replacement." I reach out to offer my hand to his partner.

"Joey Fox." He slips his clammy hand into mine and shakes it. He doesn't look well. Pulling a handkerchief from his suit jacket, he wipes his forehead

Kash checks on the man before I can. "Are you okay, Joey?"

Mr. Fox's eyes dart around the room, avoiding both of us. "Yeah, yeah, yeah," his words rush out of him. "Doing great. Never felt better."

The man isn't a spring chicken. Judging by his physical appearance alone, he's in his sixties. Kash and I both cast side-eye glances at each other. Neither of us believe the man is physically fine.

Kitty saunters in, swaying her curvy hips, and makes her way to Mr. Fox. She seems to be in no real hurry to check on his health. Considering how terrible he looks, I'm about five seconds away from calling a paramedic for him myself.

I don't miss the pissed off expression Kitty shoots in Kash's direction. I also catch the hardening of his facial features in response to her silent fuck you. Something is up between these two, and maybe even Fox. My life has given me many opportunities to be a stranger because I've been the new kid more times than I can count. But never have I felt like a complete outsider until now. They definitely share some secrets. The three of them know something I'm not privy to.

Mr. Fox launches into a coughing fit, turning red in the face and bending at the waist. A small orange bottle with a white top spills from his coat pocket, rolls across the dark hardwood floor in my direction, and stops at my feet.

I bend over to pick it up and catalog the name on the prescription bottle.

Mary Phillips.

Joey Fox isn't Mary Phillips.

I'm most concerned about the contents inside the pill bottle, but when I turn the bottle in my hand, I find the the likely culprit behind Fox's physical distress — *Oxycodone*. He must be in withdrawals.

Kitty reaches me in four strides of her long legs, snatches the bottle from me, and gives me an "eat shit and die" glare that would intimidate me if I was a lesser woman. She spins on her heel and shoves the prescription into Fox's chest. He grunts in response, but she doesn't stop to apologize or aid him in any way.

A loud sigh leaves Kash. "Get your shit together, Joey."

An unattractive and uncontrollable snort is my response. The irony is too much for me to handle. "Hey, Pot," I glare at Kash, before turning it on Fox, "Meet, Kettle."

Both men have the decency to appear sheepish rather than deny they're complete shit shows.

"I hope you get the help you need, but we need to prepare for a case. I'm sure you have pressing matters to attend to as well?" I prompt Fox to leave my temporary office. His mouth-breathing is ramping up my anxiety.

"Is this Branson Rutgers case?" Fox asks about it like he knows the client.

Kash nods his head. "Yeah, he didn't make things easy on me."

His partner doesn't seem to know when to take a hint, so I pick up a stack of case files and drop them back on the desk. "Like I said, we really should get to it."

Mr. Fox moves from foot to foot, as though he's attempting to garner the courage to say more, but he finally takes his leave. I notice that he doesn't close the door behind him.

Kash pushes a hand through the top of his hair, shakes his head, and turns for his office.

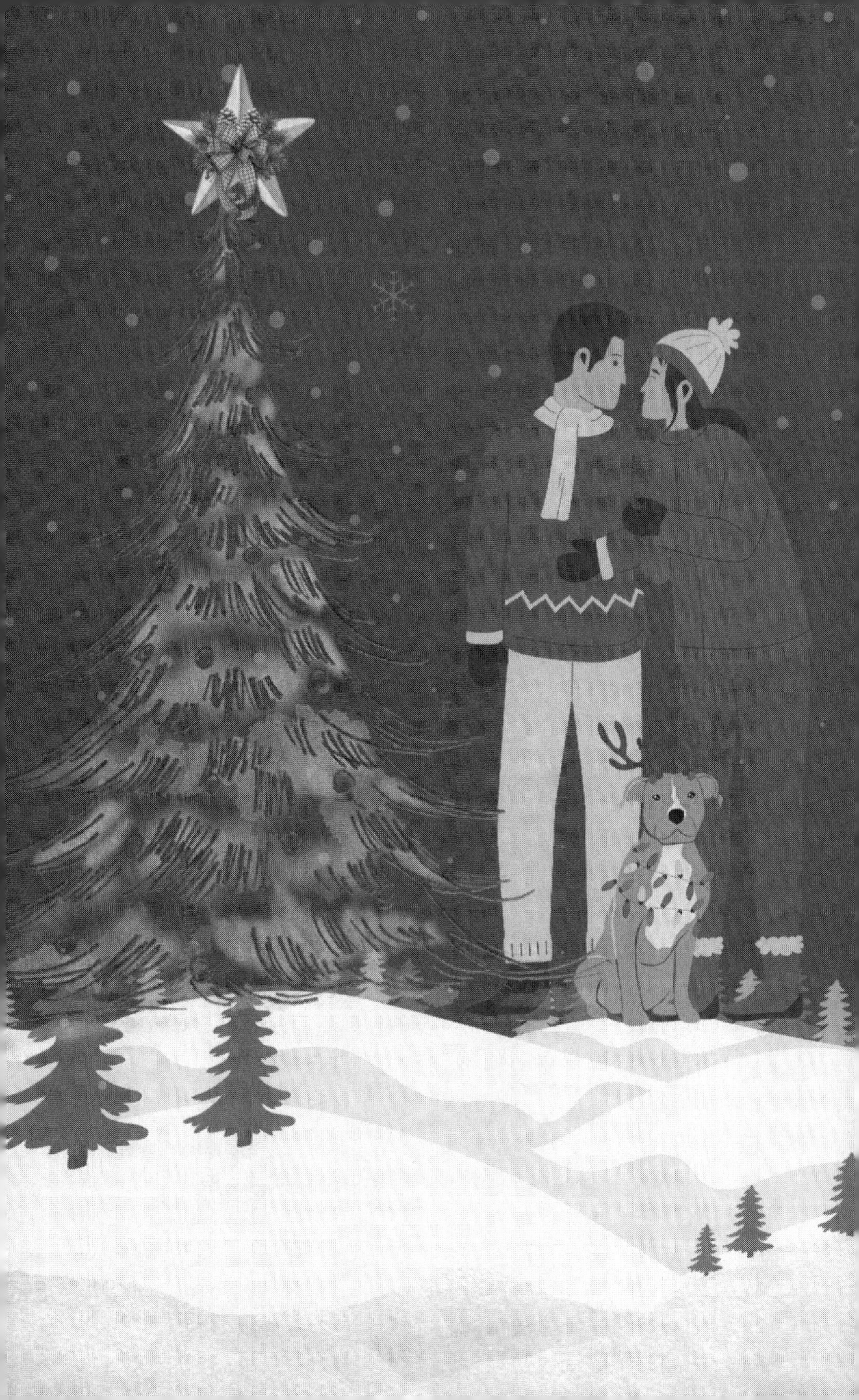

Chapter Twelve
Kash

Jesus Christ on a stick, Joey's a fucking mess. I blame Kitty for getting him hooked on pills when he threw his back out last Thanksgiving. I know I'm not one to talk, considering there was a small mountain of cocaine on my kitchen countertops two days ago. I don't let that shit consume me though. Blow is fun on the weekends, but anything beyond recreational use is sure to screw up a person's life.

Joey is a prime example of that — he's on the verge of losing his marriage and home a year before he's set to retire. I knew he was abusing pills, but I didn't know it was this bad. If he keeps it up, he's going to drag me and the firm down with him.

"The pill bottle Mr. Fox dropped belongs to a Mary Phillips," Stella says from behind me.

"Not our business." I hope she'll leave it alone, because Mary Phillips is a judge in the next town over, which means her son is probably selling any pills he can get his hands on again. The last thing I need is our firm making the paper or nightly news because Joey is eating a judge's pain medication.

"Considering he's your partner, I'd say his drug addiction and the means by which he acquires those drugs is very much your business." Her hands fly to her hips as I turn around to face her.

"I don't have time for Joey's shit today. I need to meet with Rutgers tomorrow and prepare him for mediation on Monday." I snap at her, hoping she'll drop the subject and move on. Carefully transferring myself to my office chair, I sigh with relief at being off the crutches for a while. My underarms are sore.

Stella takes one of the two burgundy, leather seats in front of my desk. She crosses one leg over the other and places her hands on her knee. "May I look through the case file while you bring me up to speed?"

Her back is straight, her shoulders are square, and her confidence shines as a result. But behind those green eyes, she holds her secrets close. It's difficult to imagine the strong, intelligent woman sitting in front of me as a domestic abuse victim.

I hand over the case file before running through the highlights. "Branson Rutgers is our client. He is being sued by Shane Williamson, his former partner for a short time. The two entered into a Joint Partnership in the State of Tennessee nine months ago for a clothing line company. Before the two could launch the gig, Rutgers quit, citing his interests lied elsewhere. He didn't violate the contract the two signed and had notarized, because Rutgers was smart enough to put in an exit clause, allowing either to vacate the partnership for any reason while also giving an appropriate amount of notice."

"Why'd he quit?" she asks the first question I had for my client.

I shrug, laying it out for her just as he did for me. "He said Williamson quit first in person but redacted his resignation. It was too late though. Rutgers didn't want to work with someone who would quit the week before the launch of their product because he can't handle the stress of self-employment."

Stella's expression is difficult to read. I can't tell which side of the fence she's going to fall on. "Okay, so Williamson is at fault for quitting and leaving Rutgers in a lurch. I don't exactly fault your client for ending it before he was to carry 100% of the weight himself. What's he suing for?"

"They had a non-disparagement agreement in their joint venture contract, but Williamson sent out an email to their customers, apologizing for dissolving the venture without notice. He was very careful with his verbiage, insinuating there was a disagreement between the two, which is false. It made Rutgers look really bad. He had no idea his partner, who had already quit, would plug a solo venture in his rush to take the spotlight off the mere fact that he can't hack it in their industry." I point to the case folder in her hands. "The email is in the file."

She sifts through the file until she comes across a copy of the correspondence. She scans the email, cringing when she reaches the appropriate sections. "Damnnnnnn. He was savage. So, Williamson quits first, but blames our client for the failure of the venture, while also not missing the opportunity to plug his solo project?"

When her gaze lifts to mine again, I'm glad she sees the error of the defendant's ways. It'll make it much easier to remind her which party is in the wrong when she meets our client. Rutgers is an asshole on a good day.

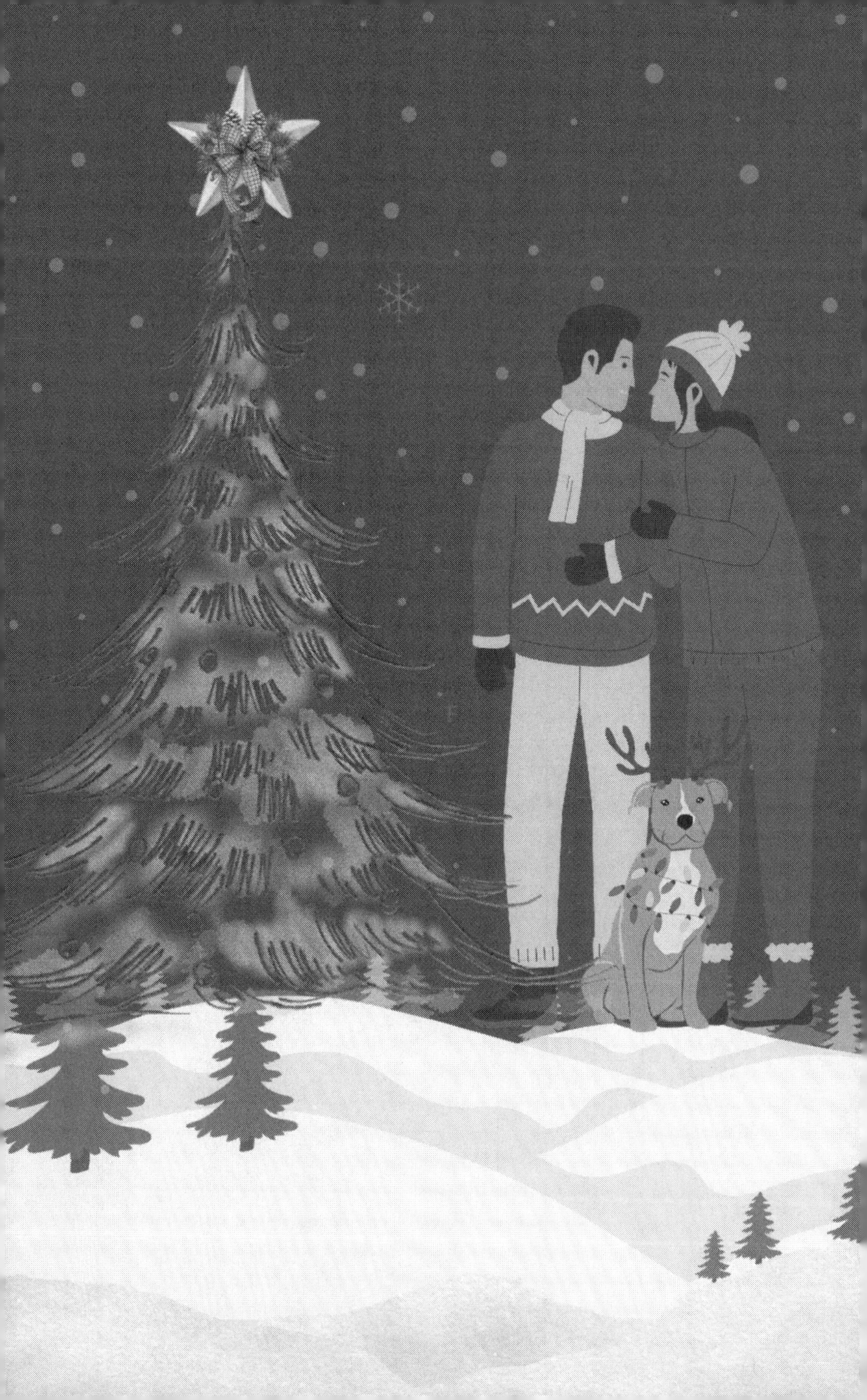

Chapter Thirteen
Stella

I take Kash up on his offer of using the apartment above his garage. The entire place is filled with dust, so I spend most of my evening after work tidying, dusting, and washing linens. I've never been able to control much about my circumstances or environment, but I can make it clean and habitable.

I haven't had my own space for most of my life. Living in foster and group homes didn't leave a lot of privacy, so I'm more than happy to have this spot, however temporary it may be.

Hours after the sun has set, a knock comes at the bottom of the staircase, which leads to a door, which divides the rest of the two-bay garage from the entrance to the apartment. Knowing Kash can't walk up the stairs, I drop the clean quilt on the bed and scurry down to answer.

"Hey." I smile as I open the door to him.

His dark brows are scrunched in a frown. "I could've been anyone."

After living with a cop for almost two years, I've heard this lecture more than once. I'm not interested in hearing it again. "But it wasn't anyone. It was you. You're the only person who knows I'm staying up here anyhow."

His blue eyes dart back and forth as he processes my retort before he grunts in final disapproval. "That's not remotely the point. You're on the run from God only knows who. Do you want to be surprised by the wrong person?"

"Okaaay!" I hold a hand up to stop him. "I hear you loud and clear. I'll ask for a code word next time."

"And what if the bad guys hear me say it?!" He throws a monkey wrench in my sarcastic attempt to appease him.

"I don't know!" I snark back at him, raising my voice to match his level. "We can use a secret knock."

"N ..." he starts to disagree with me again but stops short. "Actually, that might not be a bad idea. I'll think about a pattern."

I fight an eye roll. "We're not conducting a symphony. Knock three times, pause, knock again, pause, knock twice."

He considers my suggestion while rubbing his bearded chin. "That's a lot of knocks."

I give up with a loud sigh. "Is this why you walked all the way over here on those things?" I point to his crutches.

He looks over his shoulder at his home and crooks a thumb over it. "I ordered pizza. I thought you might be hungry after working in here all night. I'd bring it up, but yeah, stairs aren't my friend right now."

My stomach growls quietly, letting me know I need to find nourishment soon. "What kind of pizza?"

"Pepperoni and garlic — the only way to eat a pizza." His large palm flies to his belly where he rubs it in circles.

Hearing the toppings entices my salivary glands. I start drooling like a Saint Bernard. "Sounds delicious."

"Yeah?" He seems surprised by my approval in pizza topping choices.

"Let me grab my coat. It's cold tonight," I say and run up the stairs for my coat.

He's waiting on me in the same place I left him, leaning against the door jamb and peering off into the garage.

"Ready?" I break him out of his trance.

"Yeah, I'm starving." He leaves the garage, leaving me to lock up, which I take time to do, just in case.

Moving quickly after him, I catch up within a few steps. He's slow with a broken leg, so I keep pace with him to keep him from feeling rushed. My stomach growls again, but this time he can hear it.

"Christ. Thank God I thought to feed you when I did." To anyone else, he would appear worried about me. It's not the case at all. He's mentally clapping himself on the back for doing what any normal, decent person would do – remembering I exist and have needs.

I keep my opinion of my boss to myself. My purse needs the boost his $10k will provide. There's no sense in pissing him off before he hands over the funds. This is the easiest case I've ever worked. The facts are hard and fast. There's no way our client won't be awarded what he's requesting the defendant pay. I'm not sure why my help was so imperative with this case. It definitely doesn't seem like I did $10k worth of work.

Reaching the back door a few steps ahead him, I open it and stand to the side to allow him to pass through with ease. Once we're both inside, I head for the pizza box resting atop the stove.

"I'll get it. Have a seat," I offer to save him the trip.

"Thanks." The sincerity in his voice makes me falter in my step for a second.

Stop it, Stella.

I can't see any good in a man like Kash just because he's the only soul I have right now. He is what he is. It's not saying much, considering we've only known each other three days.

Retrieving the hot red pizza box from across the room, I hurry back to the table and plop the container onto the table. He uses his good leg to push a dining chair toward me. Taking it without much thought, I sidle up next to him at the table.

As soon as I open the pizza box, I realize I didn't get us plates, napkins, or silverware. Standing to take care of the tasks, he stops me by placing his large, warm hand on my thigh.

"Don't worry about it. We'll eat out of the box," he says like he didn't just set my skin on fire.

He doesn't need to know that my traitorous body has reacted to him. It's a one-off anyhow. Kashton Saint doesn't stand a snowball's chance in hell in getting into my panties.

Lowering back to the chair, I clear my throat and do my best to ignore the throb between my legs.

I need to get a grip if I'm lusting in any way, shape, or form after Kash Saint.

We eat in silence. I'm lost in a war over giving into the carnal thoughts about him. It doesn't hurt to have naughty thoughts, but I should probably avoid even a temporary employer. It's just wrong, even if I have already seen him in the buff.

"I've never had dinner here with a woman," he interrupts my ridiculous internal dialogue, gesturing around the table.

"Here at the table?" I clarify.

"No, at this house. I've fucked plenty of women on this table but never shared a meal with one." He shakes his head a second later as though he's confirming the point. "No, never."

I quickly change the subject and avoid thinking about bodily fluids underneath the pizza box. "Do you cook?"

He takes a bite of his slice, wrapping a stray piece of cheese around his finger and shoving it in his mouth. "Of course. You?"

"Yes, I can cook." I learned out of necessity, but I leave the information out.

We finish our meal. I jump to throw half-eaten crusts into the trash and tuck the leftovers inside the refrigerator. When I turn around, I find his gaze resting on me.

"What?" My anxiety ticks up a few notches with his perceptive attention on me.

"Nothing." A small smile tugs at his red lips. He turns around and lifts himself with the the help of the table. When his blue eyes land on me again, I once again note how striking he is. But it's the soft expression gracing his features that makes me look away in discomfort.

If he looks too deeply, he might see me and all my scars. He might see how utterly alone I am in this world, and it's no one's fault but my own. I hate being the center of anyone's attention, especially a stranger. It hasn't always meant good things for me in the past.

I quickly bring up the first thing that pops into my head – a nervous habit for me. "You haven't decorated for Christmas yet."

"I haven't for two years, not since my Pops died. It doesn't make much sense to decorate for just one person." He shrugs as if it's not a big deal to spend the holidays alone. "What about you? Any traditions?"

"When I was a girl, I spent a few great Christmases with my grandfather. We watched every Christmas movie ever produced, drank too much hot chocolate, and made mistletoe wishes." Fond memories tug at my heart, reminding me that I was very much loved at one point in my life.

"Mistletoe wishes?" he asks, likely confusing it with mistletoe kisses.

My entire soul fills with warmth when I remember my favorite two Christmases. "When you're alone and have no one to kiss underneath the mistletoe, you make a wish instead. You only get one wish per Christmas though, and you have to use it before midnight on Christmas."

He cocks his head to the side but is quiet for a long moment. "I like it. There's no sense in all that kissing anyhow." Kash begins to slowly make his way across the kitchen to the living room, where he plops down on a large dark brown leather sofa and releases an audible breath. "All those carbs and no gym time are going to catch up with me if I keep eating like this."

"Psh." Like he could gain an ounce. I'm pretty sure he possesses a mutant gene. Men don't look like he does in real life.

"Thank you for dinner, but I think I'll call it a night." I head toward the back door after casting a small smile in his direction.

He pops up from the couch much more quickly than someone with a broken bone should be able to, shouts in pain, and falls back to the couch, clutching his injured leg. "Fuck!"

I feel the guilt over hitting him all over again. Nothing but time will heal his injury, but it might not heal my conscience over hurting another person. Apologies spill from my mouth for harming him and for his current pain as I rush to his side. I've never been able to handle seeing a living thing in pain.

"Stella," his deep voice pulls me from my thoughts.

When I focus back on him, there's concern in his blue eyes.

"Yeah," I croak, my emotions threatening to bubble up.

"I'm okay. It's okay. You didn't do anything wrong. I just stood up on both legs like a dumb ass." He reaches for me, hesitantly touching my cheek and swiping his thumb across it.

A tear spills over my lid. He stops its path with his large thumb. I don't always feel comfortable in my own skin, especially when another person peers so deeply inside my soul. It's unnerving for him to see any of me.

"Breathe," he whispers as he searches my face.

My heart's beating in my throat. Short bursts of air leave me as I fight against my anxiety. I have to get my shit together. I can't let Darren, or my situation get the best of me. It keeps me on constant alert and in fight-or flight mode, which leads to me being a nervous, jumpy, emotional mess.

"Deep breaths, beautiful," Kash coaches me through an impending panic attack, grabbing me by my hips and pulling me closer to him.

I avoid his gaze as much as I can, but he continues to invade my space, ducking and moving to keep me focused on him. Finally, I just close my eyes and aim my attention at taking deep breaths to calm my nervous system.

"Come 'ere." Two seconds later, he picks me up and places me in his lap without even moving from the couch. Tucking my head between his neck and shoulder, he drags his fingers down my arm to comfort me. The resulting trail of goosebumps spreads from my arm to the rest of my body.

I ignore how great it feels to be held by someone while I'm struggling to merely exist. I've never had anyone invite me to be vulnerable while they held me. I've had to be tough my entire life, but I don't feel so inclined to be that at this moment.

Pulling myself together the best I can, I dry my tears and release my hold on the day.

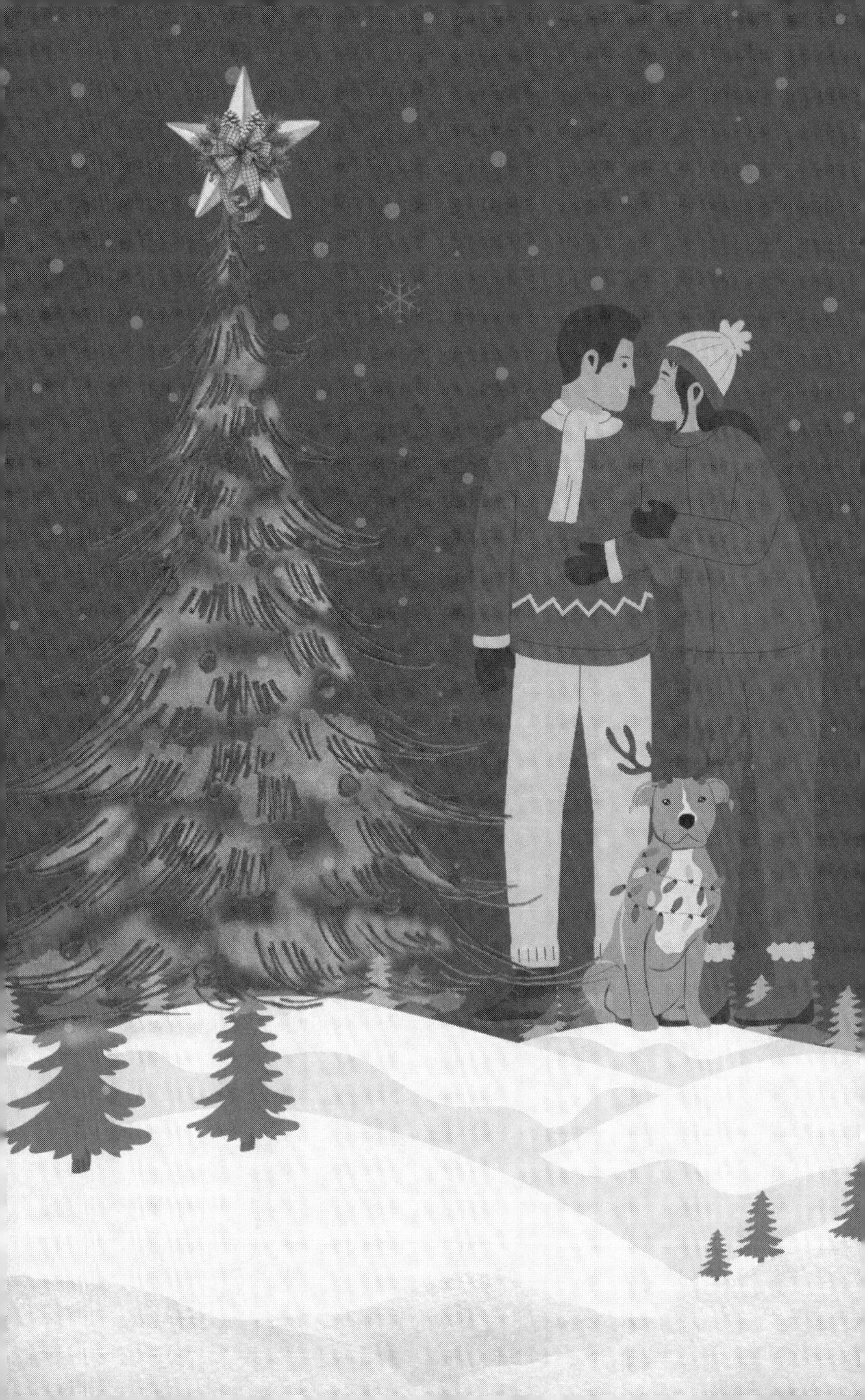

Chapter Fourteen

Kash

Rubbing my shoulder, I almost regret not moving for three hours after Stella fell asleep on my lap last night. My arm was asleep for most of that time, but it was the first time all week I'd seen Stella relax. Bothering her didn't settle well with me, but eventually, half my body ached from the position I was sitting in.

After waking her at midnight, she sleepily mumbled a few incoherent sentences, but moved toward the garage apartment. I insisted she allow me to see her across the back yard. I don't know anything about the guy who's after her, but I don't imagine he'll do nice things to her if he finds her, or else she wouldn't be on the run.

Coming back to the present, I startle as the door to my office opens, and she steps inside. "Mr. Rutgers and his family are here."

I can't read her well this morning. She's been quiet since she arrived in my kitchen earlier, where I handed her a coffee mug that I made for her before I made my own.

"Great, please show them in." I remain seated, not bothering with the crutches to meet Rutgers across the room. My fucking leg is broken, so he can come to me.

Stella hesitates at the door, opening her pretty mouth to speak, but she decides against it. She moves away from the door too quickly for me to stop her and ask what she's thinking.

Branson Rutgers is a short man with short-man syndrome. He's hard, and I'm sure he has his reasons for being the way he is. It doesn't mean I like him or the god complex he totes around with him.

He's almost a foot shorter than me, barely reaching over five and a half feet, with light brown hair that's streaked with gray. I'm more than surprised when a beautiful, leggy brunette walks in behind him with a little dark-haired boy, who is the spitting image of her. Rutgers has briefly mentioned them in previous meetings, but I only half-listen to him. The man likes to hear himself talk. His nasally voice grates on my nerves after he's exceeded the amount of words I can handle in a day.

The woman never meets my eyes, but the boy, appearing to be six or seven, peers up at me from underneath long, dark lashes. He's curious about me. His mother leans down to whisper into his tiny ear, and seconds later, he moves to a small green settee off the side of the room. Tucking his hands in his lap, he sits quietly and watches us closely. He never once cracks a smile, reminding me of myself at that age – serious but perceptive.

"May I get anyone a water?" Stella asks, picking up the part of assistant well and making our clients feel welcome.

Rutgers moves one of two chairs in front of my desk and takes the seat. Then he lifts his leg and places it on the edge of my desk, because he's an arrogant little shit. The man has more money than God, and he likes to think it makes his dick bigger. It doesn't. "I'll have a water. They're fine."

I have no idea how he snagged his wife, who comes to sit beside him, lowering gently into the seat.

Her husband never looks in her direction or speaks to her. He also doesn't introduce her, so I do it myself.

"I'd stand and introduce myself, but my bum leg makes it more difficult than usual. I'm Kash Saint, your husband's attorney." I lift a hand to gesture toward Stella. "This is my wonderful paralegal and assistant, Stella. Would you like something to drink?" If she's married to this asshole, she needs a concoction stronger than water – much stronger.

I narrow my eyes in Rutgers' direction, daring him to challenge me in my own office. He puffs his chest out, clearly agitated by my offer of a simple drink to his spouse. My amusement and glee at his anger should feel more wrong than it does.

The wife smooths down the skirt on her navy-blue dress. "Brittany Rutgers. I'd love a water. Thank you." She won't make eye contact.

Stella leaves the room to retrieve a water for Brittany and her husband, only returning with one bottle, and hands it to her instead of him. I wait for him to call her out on the subtle fuck you, but he doesn't. The wife doesn't seem to know what happened as she takes a sip of the drink.

"Your assistant said you want to prep me for mediation on Friday?" Rutgers gestures with his hand for me to move on with the reason he's here.

Fighting a grin over Stella's piss and vinegar attitude, I nod, reminding myself not to make her mad. "Yes. When you hired me a few months ago, you stated you had leverage on Williamson. Now would be a good time to share anything you know, but it's also imperative for us to hear anything he might hang over your head."

"He's involved in the kink community in Mistletoe Creek. He's supposed to be a god-fearing man. He goes to church every time the doors are open. A good Christian shouldn't be involved in these types of behaviors." The self-righteous bullshit coming out of his mouth sounds like my father.

"Christians fuck too, Branson," I not-so-subtly remind him people from all religions do the Hokey Pokey on the regular.

"Aren't you supposed to take the information and use it against him?" He grows louder by the second.

I shrug unimpressed by the information. Loathing the old glory days when a person's sexual preferences could lead to irreparable harm to their families and careers, I dig for a more useful tidbit. "What else? That can't be all you have on him."

Branson Rutgers smiles like he's Satan himself. "No. He's also having an affair with his wife's sister and has been for close to five years."

Shaking my head, I disapprove of people sharing their entire lives with each other just because they're in business together. "Bingo! That's what he doesn't want people to know or hear. Anything else?"

"No."

"What will he say about you?" Stella goes straight for the jugular, not bothering to hide the boredom in her tone.

It might just be me, but I'm almost positive she's not a fan of our client. When Rutgers shoots a glare in her direction, I intercede before he makes a stupid decision like insulting Stella. "Yes, she's right. Any dirt he has on you can be just as important as the shit you have on him. So, let's have it. What does Williamson know?"

Rutgers looks at his wife, but she's not paying attention. She's fidgeting with her wedding ring while lost in thought.

"A few years ago, I was drinking more than I should've been. I ..." he trails off, shifting in his seat and showing his discomfort. "I had too much one night and lost my temper at the dinner table." He mumbles a short sentence, but there's not any sign of remorse on his face for whatever it is he's done.

"What did you do?" I ask, knowing it must be bad if he's muttering to hide his crime.

"I hit them." His sentence is forceful as he raises his prideful chin.

Brittany stops twisting her ring around, the words pulling her from her own world, but she doesn't respond verbally. She simply looks over her shoulder at her son before hanging her head, her shame visibly weighing on her. She allowed another person to hurt her child. It may not sink in right away, or even now "a few years later", but eventually her son will resent her for staying.

Thinking of the woman who gave birth to me for the first time in a long time, I remember the bitterness I carried for most of my life along with the ghost of my mother. She loved me, as I'm sure Mrs. Rutgers loves her son, but she has to love him enough to leave the security blanket her husband provides financially. My own mother not leaving a bad man ultimately led to her death, and it was hard not to be angry at her for not picking me before he took her life.

Normally, I'd tell myself their home and marital issues don't involve me. My early memories strike a chord deep within me, sparking a visceral reaction that sneaks up on me. "When's the last time you hit either of them?"

He doesn't have to use words to reply. The guiltless, emotionless expression settling over his features tells me everything I need to know. The way Brittany sat down like it pained her to do so doesn't sit well with me. The little boy's lack of a smile that naturally graces most children's faces reminds me of me, because I know what it's like to live in hell without anyone to protect you. But his utter disregard for either of them when offered water is the biggest sign he doesn't respect them as humans with needs and fears.

I struggle deeply with what to do with Branson Rutgers. I should withdraw as his counsel, citing a huge conflict of interest, and report his ass for being an abusive asshole. Shooting a glance in Stella's direction, I tell myself she would pull herself from the case, if it were her firm or name on it. She wouldn't want to be associated with a piece of shit who abuses his wife and kid, but who does?

"I can't protect you from that." I'm honest with Branson about the reality of his situation.

He's quick to reply with a ready-made solution. "She'll say it never happened. The kid too."

Out of the corner of my eye, Stella steps closer to the boy, as though she's ready to snatch him away and protect him from both of them.

"No. I *will not* condone perjury of a domestic abuse victim just to help you recover a few grand." I put my foot down. I'm a lot of things, but this isn't one of them. I live fast and free, but I don't take away anyone's sense of safety or their ability to make their own decision, which includes using the word "no". I close his case file. "You'll need to make concessions if he decides to share that tasty morsel about you."

Branson shoots up from his chair like his ass is on fire. "You should worry about what's going on in your own backyard than what I do with what belongs to me. Try hiring a forensic accountant and see what your partner and his drug dealer have been up to." He moves over to his wife, grips her upper arm, and sneers at her. "Let's go. See what you've done now. It's always something with you or that kid."

When he pulls so hard on her she yelps, I move faster than the speed of light, forgetting about my leg again. Spilling from my chair, the entire thing flips on its side and lands on top of me. Stella pulls it off of me within seconds, but by the time I'm upright, the Rutgers have already left.

My gaze settles back on Stella, who's upset. "Who are those tears for?"

"Brittany and her son." She looks away, attempting to hide the moisture inside her pretty green eyes. "And for you. I didn't think you had it in you to be decent about ... anything. I'm sorry for misjudging you." She doesn't give me a chance to reply, turning away and leaving the room.

I consider going after her but decide to give us both a minute to process what we learned today.

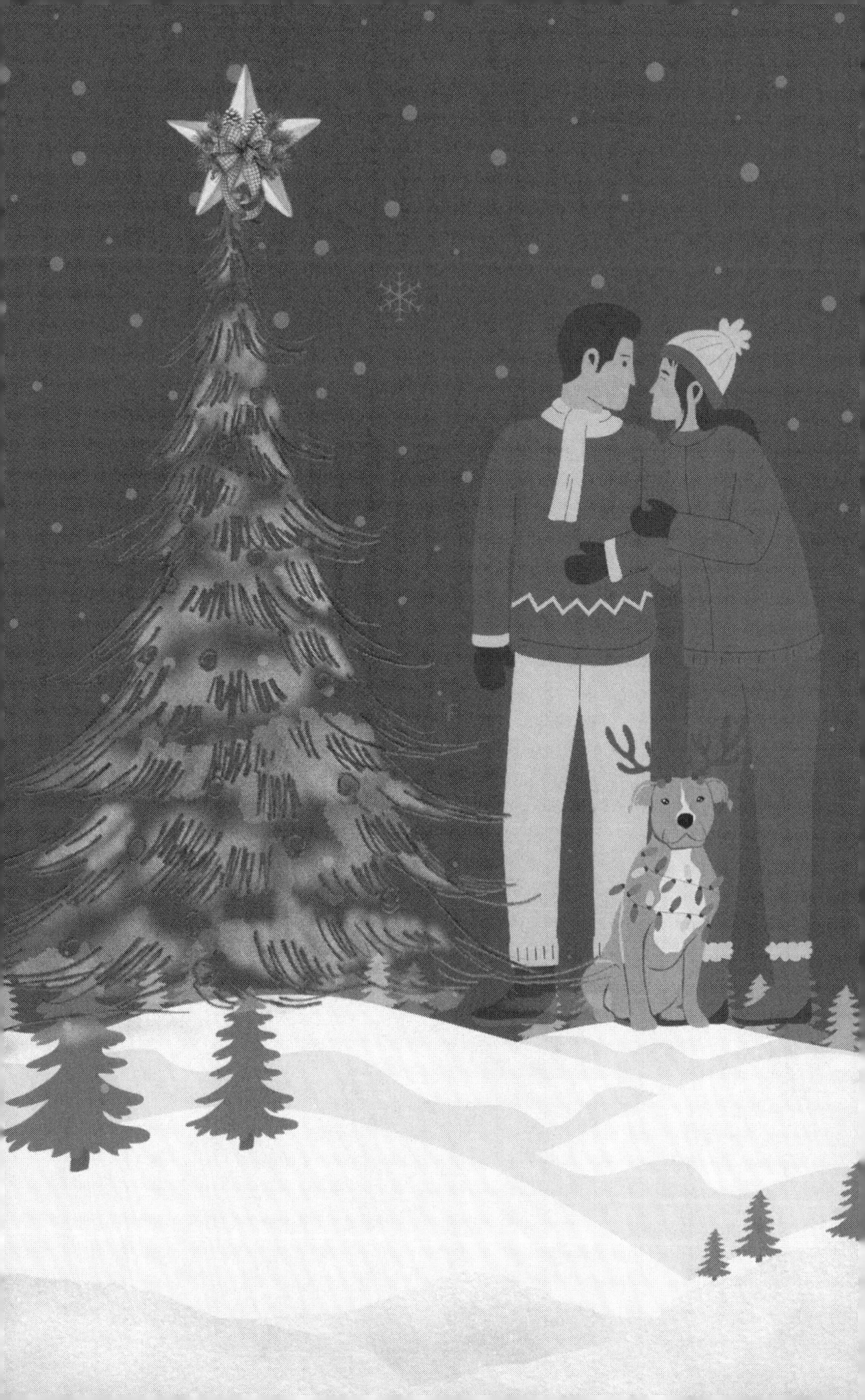

Chapter Fifteen
Stella

Stretching like a cat, I'm thankful for the weekend and a few extra hours in bed. I haven't felt this at ease in years. I also haven't been able to enjoy my weekend with literally no plans or a person controlling my every move.

Not wanting to leave the warmth of the bed, I groan but force myself out. I head to the kitchenette area for coffee but remember I don't have any grounds or the necessary milk and sugar to make it. I can always go across the back yard and ask Kash for the supplies.

I bundle up in a jacket, slip on my furry boots over my leggings, and head down the stairs. When I reach the bottom, I push through the door, leading to the garage. To my surprise, Kash is on the other side with his head buried in a blue, hard plastic tote.

"Good morning," I greet and lean against the door frame.

His dark hair is sticking up in different directions from sleep. He's wearing gray gym shorts and a black hoodie, but he looks good enough to eat. It's really unfair for a man to look the way he does with zero effort.

"Morning." He pops his head up from his task and allows his lazy gaze to travel down my body. "God bless yoga pants." He returns to the tote.

I smirk at his comment. "What are you doing?" I'm curious what he stores in the multitude of totes.

"I have tons of Christmas decorations Matilda has bought over the years." He pauses, lifts his attention to me, and motions me over. "Come and see if you like anything."

"Me?" I frown but make my way over to him.

"Yeah, we're doing Christmas today." His excitement is childlike.

I could argue against decorating, but I can't think of a better way to spend my Saturday. "You're awfully close to Christmas. It's less than ten days away."

Using his crutches, he moves to another stack of stored decorations. "Then I guess we shouldn't waste any more time."

"How much is tons?" I ask to gauge what level of Christmas we're able to accomplish today.

Kash waves an arm around the garage like he's Vanna White. "Most of this."

My jaw hits the floor. "A ton is *a lot*."

"Yes, indeed. We have a busy day ahead of us." The smile on his face is contagious.

I have nothing going on in my life, in general, except trying to stay alive. "It looks like it, but I need coffee first."

"I figured." He chuckles. "I brewed a pot before I came out here."

His small act of kindness isn't as shocking as his familiarity with my morning coffee habit. He's made me coffee every morning for a week, but he was already making it for himself, not that I'm ungrateful. He woke up on a Saturday and thought about someone other than himself, and it makes me question how wrong I might be by quickly judging him based on our first meeting.

"Thank you for making a pot. Can I make you any?" I ask, but I'm already moving in the direction of the back door.

The corners of his mouth twitch with amusement. "She's not worried about the man with a broken leg. The woman is on a mission for coffee."

"Sorry? Not sorry?" I shrug, then turn and jog across the yard.

A burst of warm air envelopes me when I step inside his home. The room smells of java and cinnamon. The scent tugs at my childhood memories as a smile blooms on my lips.

Making quick work of our coffee concoctions, I realize I don't know how he takes his coffee. His has been in a lidded mug each morning, so I can't even guess very well. Who doesn't love sugar and cream? After much internal debating, I decide to make his the exact same as mine. I can always get him another cup, if this isn't his jam.

I brave the cold December morning again, ducking out with two sage green mugs, and moan when the crisp air wraps around me. I'm ready for warmer temperatures.

Kash is moving around the garage on one crutch, flipping lids off of storage containers before he moves onto the next one. Carefully managing the maze of Christmas decorations, I reach him and hand over the mug.

"Thank you." He sips it without looking, and two seconds later, he spits the mouthful everywhere. "Holy shit, that's a lot of sugar."

I wipe the liquid from my face.

"Fuck, I'm sorry. I wasn't expecting a cup o' diabetes." He pulls his black hoodie off, rips the shirt underneath it over his head, and shoves his head back into the sweatshirt.

I don't miss the hard planes of his body, the tattoos I saw on my first day, or the way my body reacts to all the beauty on display as he hands me his shirt. Wiping my face with it, I'm hit with his cologne, which is woodsy, masculine, and spicy. I need to remove my face from it before my vagina has *ideas* about my boss.

"Thank you." I give the shirt back, avoiding his gaze, and cover my discomfort by sifting through bins he's thrown the lid from. "Where's the tree?"

"There's two. We'll put the big one in the living room. You're welcome to the small one, if you want to put it upstairs."

Weighing whether or not to tell him the truth about not being here come Christmas Day, I change the subject instead. "Is the big tree pre-lit or do we need lights?"

"It's pre-lit. I hate fighting strings of lights around a tree," he says as he slowly moves across the garage to me. "There are two boxes of ornaments over there." He points near the door to the apartment. "You're also welcome to use anything in there for your tree."

"Thank you." I don't want to ignore his kindness, but it's pointless to put a tree upstairs.

"I'll work on moving the tree and ornaments inside. It's cold out here," I remind him.

When he doesn't respond, I look over at him standing next to me and discover a frown tugging at the corners of his mouth.

"What's wrong?" I ask in a concerned tone.

"I don't like not being able to help you." The unhappiness written all over his face deepens.

Patting him on the shoulder, I reassure him. "It's okay. I broke your leg. You're forgiven."

I'm grateful when he heads inside and lets me make progress without him lingering over my shoulder.

He's pulling the Christmas tree from the box when I bring in the last bin of ornaments, so I close the space between us to help him out. He's not the greatest with balance or remembering his leg is broken in the first place.

"Hold on. Something is missing." He sticks his index finger in the air. "Elvis."

"As in the king of rock and roll?" I quirk a brow.

"As in the best Christmas album ever recorded." He winks at me.

Again, the memories of my grandfather warms me from the inside out. "Agreed."

Kash pulls his phone from his shorts and brings up a music app. Then he turns "Merry Christmas Baby" on. The King bellows from speakers located around the room, and we dive into decorating his tree.

"You have two gold ornaments too close to each other." I point to the last ornament he hangs on the tree.

Pursing his lips, he shoots me an amused, but exasperated expression. "You're one of those people."

"Do you want to stare at two gold ornaments or a nicely decorated tree with equally spaced colors and ornaments?" I ask, not understanding how anyone can decorate a tree haphazardly. There should be rhyme and reason to the pattern.

His eyes widen before he throws his head back and laughs. "Breathe, Stella. It's not that serious. I can see your mind working a mile a minute over this."

Embarrassment heats my cheeks. "I didn't have control over most of my childhood, so my brain attempts to control what it can. Sorry."

He grows quiet, but I ignore the heaviness suddenly filling the air. "Me too." His voice is barely above a whisper.

I don't respond. We all have fucked up childhoods and wear the scars it leaves behind. I don't rate trauma. No one's pain is more significant or more important than another's. Not wanting to engage in a conversation where we compare battle wounds, I change the subject. "The tree looks great. We did a good job."

"Yeah, we did." His tone is sad.

I avoid digging for the reason behind it. "I'll just head back to the apartment. I should gather my laundry and —"

He cuts me short. "But you haven't had any hot chocolate yet." Before I have a chance to reply, he moves to the kitchen with the help of his crutches. "Did I mention it's gourmet hot chocolate?" he asks when he reaches the island in the middle of the room, flipping the box over to read its ingredients. "Organic, too."

"You play dirty." I narrow my eyes at him, but I follow him to the kitchen, snatching the box away from him when I reach him.

"The woman loves her sugar," he mutters, but he doesn't hide his amusement.

"Shush." I fight a smile.

I bring the ingredients and mugs to the island, and we work together to pour the milk over hot chocolate powder.

"Let me put these in the microwave." Leaving him behind, I double-fist the mugs and carry them across the room to heat them. When I turn around, Kash is staring into the living room. "What is it?"

His gaze flickers over to me. "We did a jam-up job on the tree. What should we decorate next?"

"You want more Christmas?" I don't mean to sound so surprised.

He shrugs. "Yeah. It makes me happy to be surrounded by the Christmas spirit, I suppose."

When the drinks are done in the microwave, I carry them back to Kash. "Your hot chocolate, sir."

"Thanks." He takes a big gulp of it, wipes his hot chocolate mustache from his mustache, and swipes his tongue across his bottom lip. "Wow. This has to be the best hot chocolate I've ever tasted."

I follow suit, placing the mug to my lips and drinking down the warm goodness. My eyes roll back in my head, and a moan slips out. "You tell no lies."

He chuckles. "She says to the attorney." Reaching out to me, he wipes residue from above my lip. "You just have a little …"

"Oh? Thank you." My body responds so easily to Kash's unexpected touch, I have to avert my attention away in hopes he doesn't notice.

Clearing his throat, he moves us past my discomfort. "Why don't we bundle up, and we'll head back to the garage for the next project?"

We're in the garage for another fifteen minutes, but we uncover the rest of the décor and organize it in stacks before selecting garland and wreaths as our next task. Kash grumbles again about not being able to move the boxes, but I manage it easily enough without his help.

When I come in with the fourth and final box of greenery, he's leaning against the door frame that separates the kitchen from the living room. His blue eyes follow me across the space, and when I reach him, he lifts his gaze to the threshold where mistletoe combined with holly and twine dangles from a small nail.

"Have you made your mistletoe wish this year?" he asks and lowers his attention back to me.

"No. You only get one, remember?" I answer, but I release the laugh bubbling up at his remembering a detail from my childhood ramblings.

"You're not a gambler." He points out the obvious.

"No."

"So, you take your time with the wish to ensure it's the right one. Do you wait until the very last minute to make it?" His curiosity is hard not to give in to.

"It depends on the year and what's happening in my life." I'm honest without being too detailed about the holidays I've spent beaten, battered, and hungry.

"Fair enough." He pauses, lifts a brow, and asks, "What did you wish for last Christmas?"

Hesitating to share a wish is silly, but the question stops me in my tracks for a long moment. "To be safe, healthy, happy, and full the next Christmas."

His masculine, handsome features soften. "You left out four imperative points in your wish – hot chocolate, decorations, Elvis, and Christmas movies."

"It's okay. You don't have to watch Hallmark movies with me." I giggle at this being the same man who I met butt naked in his kitchen a week ago.

"What?" He puffs his chest out. "You don't think I can handle Hallmark movies?"

"Oh, there's no way you can handle it." I shake my head while wearing a doubtful expression. "Guaranteed to make even the most macho man cry."

He considers me for a beat before sticking his hand out. "Deal."

"What?" I squeak, not sure if *I* can handle a tearful Kash, because he's sure to have moisture in those pretty blue eyes.

Moving from underneath the mistletoe, he almost glides to the couch. He's gotten much faster on the crutches. "Let's do it to it then."

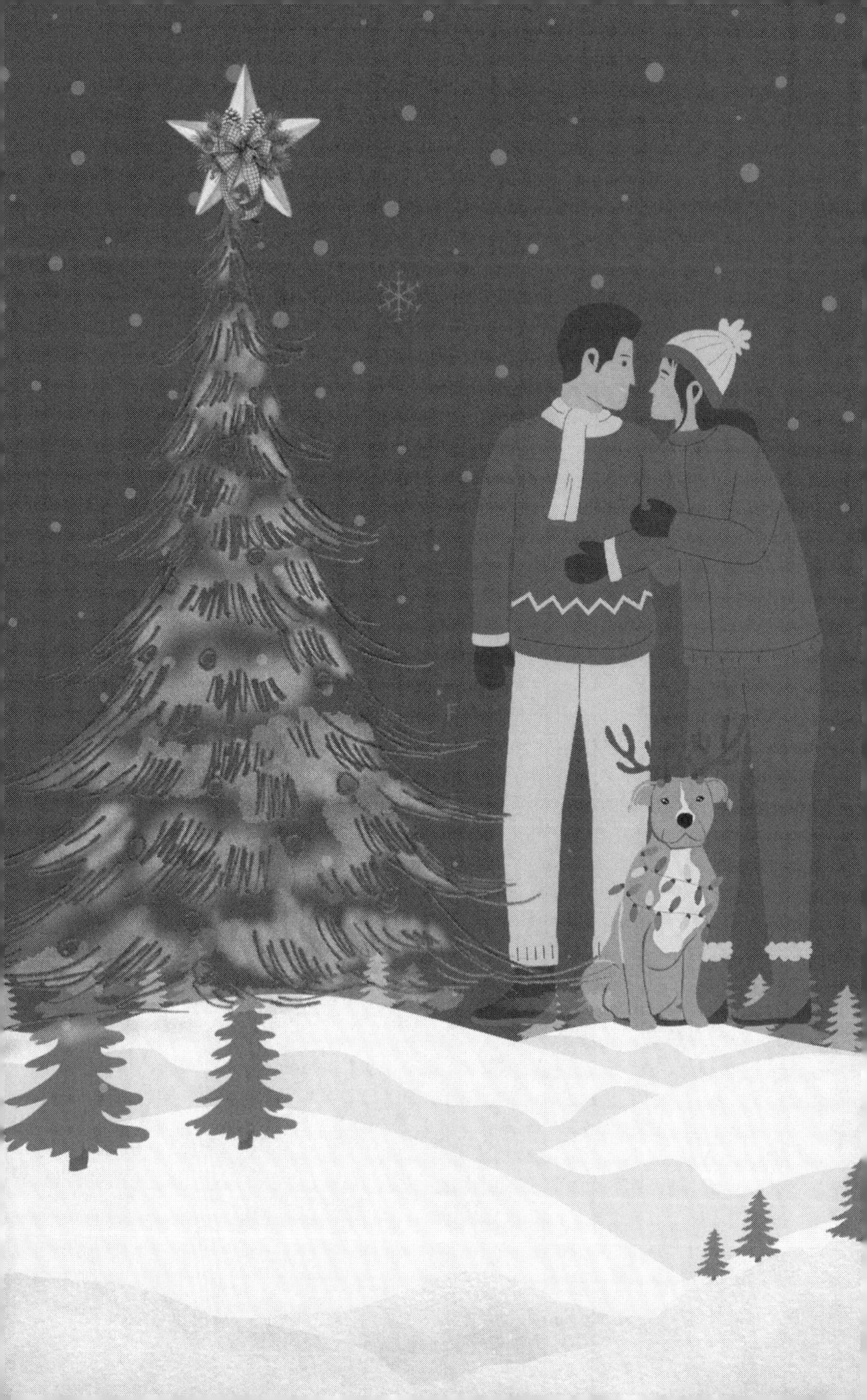

Chapter Sixteen
Kash

Watching a movie titled "Underneath the Mistletoe", I dive into the deep end of a Hallmark Christmas romance with Stella. My attention span makes it more difficult to focus when she sits on the other end of the couch from me. It piques my interest because she usually prefers her seats to be singles, where others can't get too close.

After several attempts to distract her, she shushes me without lifting her gaze from the TV.

"It's getting to the good part," she says, but I'm not sure I believe her. She suddenly sits straight as a board and points to the picture. "Look at the puppy!"

I love dogs, so it gets my attention. The female main character is crying and holding a golden retriever pup. The male main character tied a red ribbon around the critter's neck. As the camera zooms in on the silky ribbon, I lean in closer, waiting for the cheesiest shit of all time to happen while silently predicting what the dude tied to the dog.

I bet it's a key, as in the key to his heart.

Cheese central.

"Awwwww," Stella's voice is full of emotion.

I abandon the stupid movie in favor of watching her. "He hasn't unveiled it yet. Why are you already crying?"

Heat creeps into her cheeks. "Because I remembered what happens next."

Shaking my head at her, I smirk. "Why do you cry during a movie you've seen before?"

Stella worries her plump bottom lip before answering me but never makes eye contact. "Because he gave her the key to his heart."

I laugh. "I knew it! So cliche and predictable."

"Maybe so, but it's also romantic. He wants her to have the key to his heart because she's never had a home. She now has one with him, wherever he is, forever and always." She wars with emotion throughout her entire reply.

I don't know if it's the words she uses or if it's seeing her so upset, but my chest tightens in the middle.

The movie hits home for her. It's why she's crying, and the fact that she's endured whatever she has to land her pretty ass on my couch, endears her to me. The poor woman is on the run from only God knows who, but she still has enough compassion and empathy to cry for a fictional character's happily ever after.

She dries her eyes then leaves the couch. "I'm heading outside to find more decorations."

She wants a moment alone, so I give it to her, but I don't let her out of my sight. I move over to the window and watch her closely as she picks through Christmas decorations. I find Stella fascinating, but I can't put my finger on what it is that keeps me staring at her for over twenty minutes. Her expressions are plentiful, morphing from one face to another. She wears her heart on her sleeve, not doing a very good job of hiding her true feelings on any given matter. In the span of six days, I've come to enjoy almost everything about the woman – she's smart, beyond beautiful, and so strong, whether she realizes it or not.

I tear myself away from the kitchen window when she picks up a box and heads back inside, greeting her at the door to open it ahead of her arrival.

"What did you find this time?" I ask, sincerely interested in the pieces that tickle her fancy.

"There's an entire village of the cutest freaking houses in here! They've never been opened." She sets the box down by the couch and mimes an explosion with both of her hands. "Insane. I always wanted to piece together a village, so I'm not passing up this opportunity." Cocking her head to the side, she peers up and off to the right. "Hmmmmm."

It's the way her entire face lights up with glee, the smile blossoming across her delicate features, and the way she touches her chest when something is significant to her that locks my stare on her. I have no idea how I know all this about a woman I've known for six days, but there it is.

She's complex and complicated at the same time with so many layers it'd take a lifetime and another to get to the bottom of her. I should steer clear of her, but the nostalgia of the holiday tugs at my heartstrings. Spending Christmas with a beautiful, kind stranger in my bed is much more enticing than spending it alone … again.

Cataloging the types of little houses she's unearthed, Stella rambles about the things we need to complete her dream village. Nothing would make me happier than bringing it to life for her. Later, when I'm alone, I can ask myself what the fuck I'm doing with my life right now. I'm not the type of guy who helps random chicks build Christmas villages in my home.

The Christmas lights on the tree twinkle in her green eyes every time she turns her head to speak directly to me. When she's not a nervous, uptight wreck, it's easier to see the person beneath all the anxiety. Even in the middle of a terrifying time in her life, Stella finds joy in decorating my home, not once asking to take any of it to her apartment.

"You could take them up to the garage with you." I offer without thinking twice about it, because I know she'll appreciate it far more than I will.

She considers it but shakes her head. "There's not enough room or countertops for all of these."

"You can make a smaller village with the space you do have." I suggest, hoping she'll make the space her own for her duration here.

She gasps. "What? And break up the village? It'll be too spectacular as one piece to separate the pieces."

Amusement fills me. "Psh. What was I thinking?"

Her eyes are full of humor. "I'm glad you see the error of your ways."

Stella is, hands down, classically beautiful with green cat eyes and full, pouty lips. She has the girl next door vibe working for her. There's a certain innocence in her eyes that appeals to me, but I'll be damned if I know why. I imagine her being shy sexually, and that isn't my usual M.O., not by a long shot.

I watch her while she constructs the perfect village on my mantle and around the massive stone fireplace in the center of the room. She's perfectly content to work in silence, singing Christmas carols as she goes. There's a simplicity to the happiness I find in being her spectator, absorbing every expression on her pretty face.

When she nears the end of the box of houses and shops, I decide to reward her for all the hard work, and gourmet hot chocolate makes her smile. Grunting, I manage to rise from the couch and amble toward the kitchen. Stella is in her own world, so I don't interrupt her process until two mugs of chocolate goodness are ready.

She catches me by surprise when she sidles up beside me at the kitchen island. "I smell hot chocolate."

"I swear you could join the K-9 unit if they ever need to shake down diabetics smuggling sugar." I laugh at her love of sugar.

She giggles as she lifts a mug to her lips and moans in delight, her eyes rolling back in her head. The moan and eye roll fuck me up on so many levels. My dick twitches in my pants. It's been almost a week since I've had sex, and it's what I tell myself is the entire reason behind my arousal.

"Mind taking mine to the couch for me?" I ask, hoping to send her ahead of me to allow me time to adjust my junk.

"Yeah, sure." Fortunately, she's oblivious.

I grumble about my leg being a cockblock on the way to join her, but thankfully, she doesn't pay me any mind. Reaching the couch, I plop down next to Stella, and secure the crutches against the end of the sofa.

Quiet stretches between us as we both admire her work on my fireplace.

"It needs a train and tracks," she murmurs to herself before sipping her drink.

"I can't agree more. It would be perfect with the addition of a train." My focus isn't on the village any longer. It's on the beauty next to me. "We'll find one after dinner."

Stella's eyes widen with joy as she turns her attention on me. "Seriously?"

Lifting a shoulder like it's not a big deal or completely out of character for me, I attempt aloofness. "Sure. Why not?"

I don't expect her to bounce in her seat or throw her arms around me and place a kiss on my cheek. "You're the best!"

How could a man hurt a woman so sweet and kind? The more comfortable she grows here, the more her personality shines. She's nothing like the women I spend my time with – fast, easy, and superficial. Stella shouldn't appeal to me, but here I sit, with a boner from a simple hug. It's not my usual reaction.

Maybe, I should take a breather for a few hours under the guise of a nap before I do something extremely stupid. I can't fuck Stella until this case is over, if then. I've never been scared to make a pass at a woman.

Before I can leave the couch and exit the room, she draws me in with the hope in her voice. "Do you want to watch another Christmas movie?"

"No more Hallmark movies. I can't handle the cheese level." I laugh when she pokes her bottom lip out in protest, but it's a nervous reaction to the way my chest tightens at her disappointment.

"No worries. There are plenty of other movies to choose from. How about 'The Grinch'?"

"Why that movie?" I'm curious why it's her first pick.

She leans her head to the side. "He was misunderstood. It's nice to see that he could learn to love and also learn to allow others to love him back."

Her words hit closer to home than I'm comfortable admitting to myself. Some of the people in Mistletoe Creek treat me like an outsider because I wasn't born here. It probably wouldn't have been as bad if I hadn't also been a foster kid the town Scrooge adopted. My father didn't teach me how to love in a traditional, nurturing way. He was a hard man, who often saw things in black and white. Gepetto never hurt me, but his extremely high expectations were impossible to meet. I often rebelled instead of admitting I was scared to try and fail him, but I toed the line at times too, attending law school like he did. I hated law school, but I've never seen him happier to have a discussion with me.

Did I ever truly let him love me? See me?

Shaking the thoughts of my old man from my mind, I refocus on Stella. "What's choice number two?"

The concern she's wearing for me forces my gaze away. She doesn't need to *see* me or the scars I carry.

"I think we should spend time with the Griswold's," she says and slides her hand over mine, resting beside me, to comfort me.

"Sounds good." My tone is short and gruff. I hope it's enough to hide the emotions overwhelming me.

When she doesn't respond, I flick my eyes back to her. She's locked onto me, doing her best to read the shift in my mood.

Dragging the tips of her fingers between mine, she glances down for a second. "I'm sorry if I upset you." Her voice cracks over the last word.

"Hey," I soften my tone, lift my hand from underneath hers, and tuck her chin between my thumb and index finger as a lone tear rolls down her cheek. I wipe it away with my free hand. "You didn't do anything but bring me happiness today. I've immensely enjoyed the hot chocolate and decorating."

When did I become so fucking honest? Or affected by a woman's tears?

She won't give me her eyes, and it bothers me. I pick her up and move her into my lap. Her being upset can't possibly be because I had a moment.

"What's wrong? Talk to me." I encourage her to share so she'll feel better. It would also give me an idea of how I can help.

She waves it off as she wipes her eyes. "Nothing. I'm just emotional during the holidays as it is, and my current situation is likely just compounding it." She weakly attempts a smile. "I'll get out of your hair so you can enjoy the rest of your Saturday."

I don't believe her for a second. She tries to leave my lap, but I grip her by the hips and pull her back down to me. "Don't go while you're upset."

"It can't feel great for me to put my weight on your thigh." She sniffles, arguing against being in my lap. She moves to leave again, but this time she throws her leg over me, momentarily straddling my lap.

"Don't worry about me." My hands lower a hair, holding her by the hips and in place.

What the fuck am I doing?

I'm slightly terrified to look at her, but when her breath hitches, it pulls my gaze to her. Her green eyes are on me. Her lips are parted, and her breasts heave up and down with deep intakes of air.

I wage a fucking war inside of myself on whether I should release her and take a cold shower or take her right here in the middle of my living room. Where's the mistletoe when a man needs to make an emergency wish? Except, I'm not sure what I'm wishing for yet – to get hot and sweaty with Stella or for her to find safety and freedom. She deserves a guy who'll give her Christmases, hot chocolates, and trains.

"Kash." The lust in her voice is unmistakable. "We shouldn't ..." she trails off.

We shouldn't do anything requiring this position, but Jesus Christ, she has me coiled tightly with arousal. A cold shower would save me if I could snap my fingers and be there, but there's no hiding the erection beneath her if I have to walk across the room.

Closing my eyes, I release her hips so she can leave. I don't always make the best decisions, but this is one of those times. I'd lose sleep over whether or not I took advantage of her situation.

Stella shifts to move off my lap, so when her soft, warm lips touch mine, I'm more than a little shocked. My eyes fly open, my hands return to her lower back, and I lean into the kiss just a bit. She parts her lips, so I follow suit. I don't kiss women, but apparently, I kiss Stella.

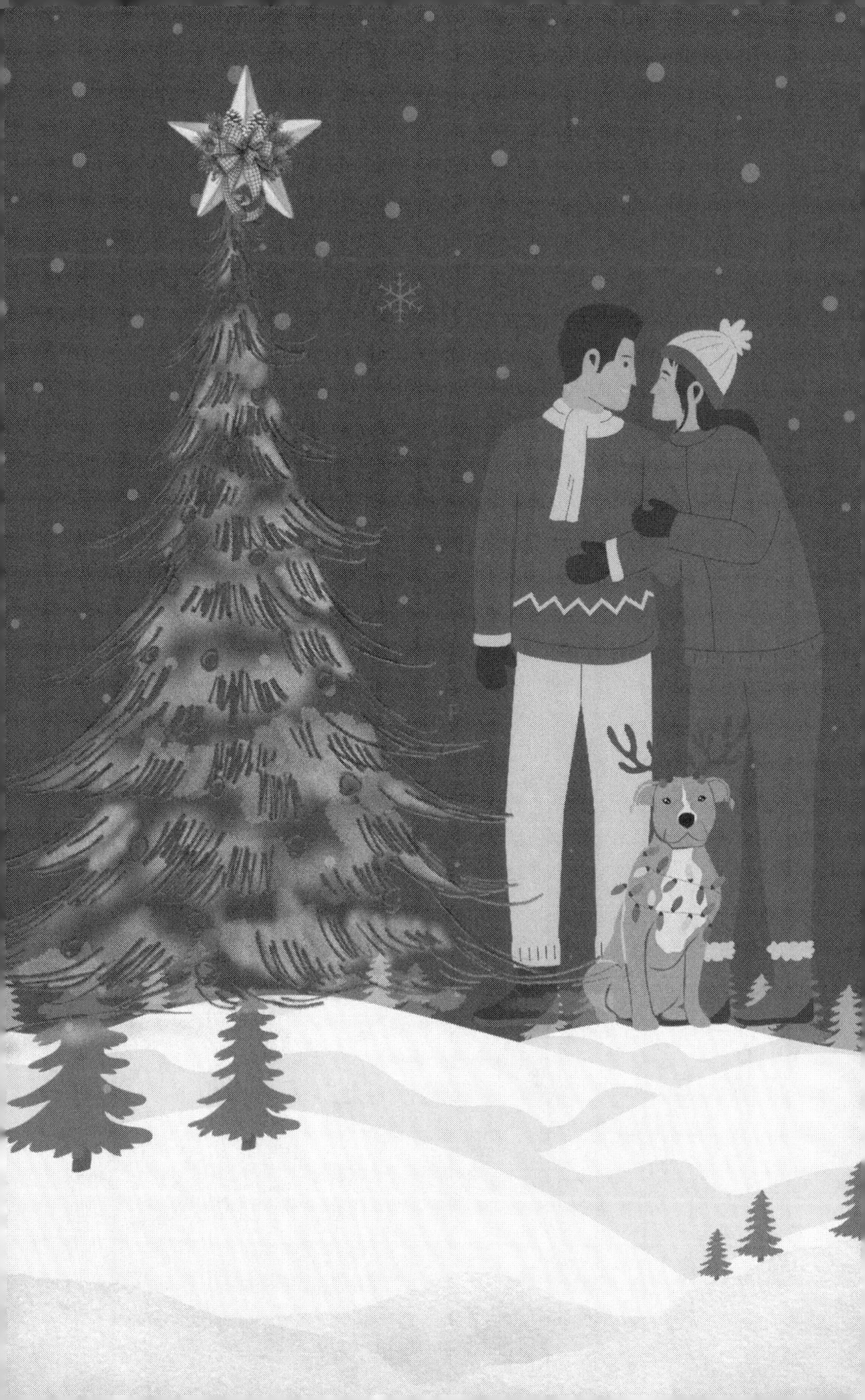

Chapter Seventeen
Stella

Kash's beard touches my face as he deepens the kiss, and ... What the hell am I doing with him?

I'm about to gather my bearings and reclaim my sensibilities, but his warm lips touch mine again and a deep moan escapes him. I'm not sure if I've ever heard a man moan quite like him. I most certainly have never enjoyed the simple act of hearing someone's pleasure or the pure satisfaction over being the reason for it.

His tongue hesitantly slips in between my lips, tasting of chocolate and something uniquely him. He's uncertain of himself, moving stiffly, at first, but he leans his head to the side and dives inside me. Kash opens me wide and swims inside my depths – slowly and thoroughly.

My body reacts to the stimulation with my nipples pebbling, my center growing wetter by the second, and my breath getting heavier.

He grunts and slides his hands underneath my shirt. They travel up the side of my ribs, leaving a trail of goosebumps in their wake. I arch my back but have no real control over the response.

Breaking our kiss, he sits back against the couch and looks at me from underneath hooded lids. His blue eyes are hazy with lust. "This is where you stop me."

There's a plea in his tone, but his large palms continue to glide along my skin as if they aren't listening. "Your skin is so soft."

I haven't been touched like this … well, ever. Darren never showered me with affection or handled me in a sweet and gentle manner. His touch didn't set my entire soul on fire. I was attracted to him, but he didn't warm my entire body with just a kiss.

I don't know what possesses me to reach for the hem of my shirt and pull it over my head. My self-consciousness creeps up on me. I cross my arms over my black bra. Shyness overtakes me, making it difficult to make eye contact with him.

He leans forward, presses his lips to the center of my chest, and peppers kisses up to my throat, chin, and finally, my lips. His fingers slip underneath the strap of my bra, unhook the clasp, and push it down my arms. Leaving one large palm against the middle of my back, he uses his other to cup my breast and leans in to lick my nipple. A moan that doesn't even sound like me climbs up my throat and somersaults out of my mouth.

"Fuck, the way you sound." He lifts his face from my chest and levels me with an intense expression. Lowering his eyes to my breasts again, he smiles. "You have the prettiest pair of tits I've ever seen."

It takes great effort not to blush and behave like a schoolgirl in front of him. He's … *experienced*. Comparatively, I'm practically a virgin. There's no way I can keep up with a guy like him sexually.

"You're overthinking," he calls out to me, bringing me back to the present.

"You pay entirely too much attention to me." I sigh and think twice about my decision to take my clothes off with Kash.

He frowns. "I don't think I've ever heard a woman say that. And why wouldn't I? You're beautiful."

I've never been great at accepting compliments, but I let my graciousness lead. "Thank you." I look everywhere but at him.

"Hey." His voice is soft. "You don't have to hide from me. You shouldn't hide from anyone. Be you, Stella, and stop caring about what other people think." He grabs my hand and places it on his crotch. "This is a sure sign the man you're with wants to see all of you."

Turning over his words in my head, I realize how silly I'm being about my body. I'm not a teenager. I have nice enough curves, but I've never been comfortable in my own skin. What do I have to lose by sleeping with him? No one has to know, and it's not like he's going to shout it from the rooftops.

Still, I'm naked in more ways than one right now. I don't want to feel that way anymore, so I lean forward and kiss him again. I need him to focus on how I *feel* rather than how I *look*. He returns the kiss, maintaining a slow, passionate pace, but I'm not interested in slow.

Tugging at his hoodie, I help him escape it, then attack him. Pressing my lips to his, I speed up the tempo, rubbing my palms across the planes of his muscular chest and wishing I could pause our kiss long enough to look more closely at his ink. If I stop what I'm doing though, I could lose my courage all together.

"Take your pants off," I murmur against his lips as I tug at the top of his gym shorts, my rushed words relaying the urgency for him to do so.

"Need a condom. Look in the drawer under the knives in the kitchen."

I leap off him and run into the next room, so he doesn't have long to look at me in the nude. I ignore the burn of his stare into my skin, and instead, fixate on why a man would store condoms in his kitchen. Putting it out of my mind, I quickly return to him, finding him completely nude with his gym shorts around his ankles. I saw his dick the morning we met days ago, but he wasn't hard.

"That might not fit," I warn him.

"It'll fit," he's quick to assure me. "You're overdressed." He slips his fingers into the top of my leggings and pushes them over my ass and down my legs. "And if it weren't for this fucking leg, I'd undress you all the way and carry you to my room. For that, I apologize."

Groaning at not being able to experience that, I remove my leggings. When I'm free, he guides me to his lap again. He makes quick work of the condom. He doesn't line himself up like I expect, but instead, slides a finger between my folds.

"Christ, you're wet." He explores me, rubbing my arousal around my clit, but he never takes his eyes off me. Inserting two large fingers, he plays my body like a violin. My back arches and my legs begin to shake when he touches the most sensitive spot on my body. Just when I'm about to fall apart, he stops. It's like hitting a brick wall at ninety miles per hour.

He doesn't give me time to protest though, because he lines himself up and thrusts up. It's just enough friction to make me want more. I sink down on him, allowing my body a few seconds to adjust to his size. Then I work my hips back and forth, slowly, at first, but with each hiss, moan, and word of praise that leaves him, I lose my mind. I forget to make it last, because he feels better than anything I've ever experienced.

Kash makes several attempts at slowing me down, but then he places a kiss in the right place or scrapes his teeth across the sensitive flesh of my neck, and I lose sight all over again. My body begs for release with each buck of my hips and each thrust of his.

"Good girl," he praises when I lean my head back and give myself over completely.

We're a tangle of limbs, kisses, teeth, and sweat moving in sync as though we've done this a thousand times before with each other. I'm on the precipice of release for a small eternity when he leans back himself and changes the angle.

"Oh, God," I cry out as my eyes roll back in my head.

"Come for me, Stella," he commands, and it's almost enough to push me over the edge.

I meet him thrust for thrust until my skin prickles from ecstasy and my orgasm washes over me. My eyes close as I surrender to it, allowing its waves to consume me wholly. I never want to come back down to earth, because this moment in time is the best physical feeling I've ever experienced.

"That's a good girl," he whispers into my ear, taking over as I collapse against his shoulder in a heaving, sweaty mess.

Kash's hands remain on my hips, pushing and pulling me on top of him. It takes a moment to recover, but it happens much more quickly than usual. The moment I'm completely coherent again, I sit up, somehow not thoroughly sated with him still moving inside me.

"She's greedy," he says moments before he moves a hand and presses it behind my head to guide me closer to his mouth, where he kisses me hard and deep. "I need you to come again. Watching you fall apart is better than it happening to me." There's reverence in his voice, but ignoring it is best.

I can't share an emotional connection with King Ding-a-ling. He's not capable of bonding with anyone, other than Matilda, who kept him on the tit too long.

"Come back." He places a sweet kiss on my chin.

The sugar in his voice gives me pause, but I also ignore it, continuing to move on top of him at the same punishing pace.

The tips of his fingers dig into my skin. "Slow down so I can feel you."

I'm not a selfish person, in general, and I try to be a thoughtful lover, so I want him to find his release more than I want another one for myself. Slowing down won't help me accomplish a second orgasm, but I do it anyhow to fast forward to the ending, where he fills the condom. I'll return to the apartment and bury my shameful self in the pillows.

It's not what happens though. He takes his sweet time, touching every last inch of my body, frequently changing the angle as best he can in this position. His watchful eye never leaves my face and body, seemingly enjoying the act of watching me. Our lips meld together as I begin my fall again. I come so hard the second time, colors dance across my vision, temporary deafness falls on my ears, and my body stiffens with overwhelming pleasure.

The second I begin to regain my senses, he erupts inside of me. The head of his cock swells and twitches as he shouts my name in ecstasy. His beautiful blue eyes squeeze shut, and the space between his brows draws together. "Oh, fuck! Stella, fuck!" Shivering beneath me, the muscles in his chest and arms quiver from exertion. His warm breath dances across my neck, and his large palm traces an invisible path from the top of my spine to the very bottom of it.

The last thing I remember is him whispering to me as the winter sun begins to set in the sky. "Come 'ere." He wraps his arms around me and hugs me tightly, pressing light kisses along the top of my shoulder.

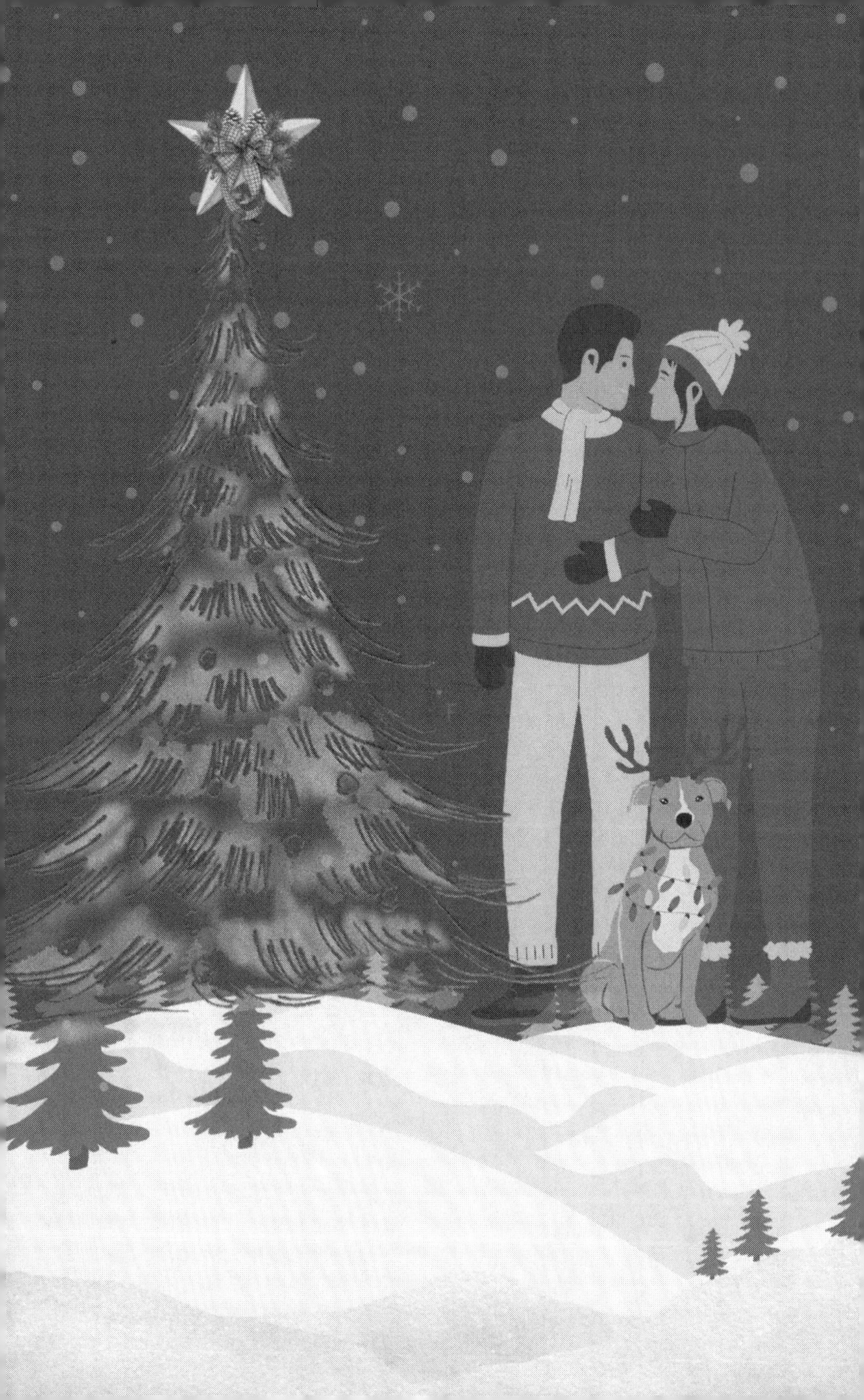

Chapter Eighteen
Kash

The morning sunlight filters through the windows and wakes me up. I move before opening my eyes and immediately regret it. My neck and shoulders scream in protest from sleeping next to Stella on the couch all night.

My eyes pop open.

Stella.

Fuck.

I didn't.

Oh, I most certainly did.

A devilish grin spreads across my lips.

"Stella?" I call out to her, hoping she's already on top of brewing coffee.

"No, but I'd love to know where she got off to." A man says from behind me in my kitchen.

"What the fuck?" I sit up on the sofa. My gaze darts around the room until it lands on a perfect stranger. "Who the fuck are you?"

"Lieutenant Darren Peoples." He flashes a badge, but I can't scope its authenticity out from here.

Sighing, I collect my crutches and heave myself from the couch cushion. I catch a whiff of Stella's scent when I pick my hoodie up from the floor and slip into it.

She was against me for several minutes before I took it off. Or maybe, I smell her from where she laid against my chest all night.

"Let me guess, you're the shithead ex-boyfriend who likes to knock her around sometimes. Did I get that right?" I prod to get a reaction.

The closer I move toward him, the more I hone in on his features. His nose has been broken from the looks of it – crooked and bumpy. I silently hope Stella broke it at least once. His light brown hair is slicked back like he lives in the wrong era.

"Listen, Fonzie," I pause when I reach him, spitting at his feet, "You aren't welcome in Mistletoe Creek. You definitely aren't welcome in my home. Your badge won't protect you from me and what I'm going to do to your career. Don't get me started on what I'll do when I fry your ass and rip your badge away. I'm sure I can arrange your stint in a maximum-security prison. They always need more pussy to go around in those places."

He lifts a gun, pointing it directly at my gut, and sneers. "I don't know what Stella told you, but she's a lying bitch. She's not mentally okay. I've been looking for her. When your assistant did the background check on her, it triggered multiple agencies who have been on her trail. We just want to make sure she gets the help she needs."

Matilda wouldn't have conducted a background check as part of her interview, so disbelief settles over my face. "Then where are those agencies and why are you pointing a weapon at me?"

"I found her!" I hear a feminine voice shout from the back yard.

Looking out the window, I find Kitty with a handful of Stella's dark hair. They struggle from the garage toward the house, but Stella fights her every step of the way. While Darren is watching it unfold, I take the opportunity to pick up my crutch and swing it as hard as I can at his head.

The gun discharges, scaring me shitless, as he drops like a sack of potatoes. Looking to see if I've been hit, I don't have a moment to find my calm when Kitty and Stella burst through the back kitchen door.

Stella's green eyes are wide as they travel down my body, back up, and down again.

"I'm okay," I reassure her.

When her bottom lip quivers, I know I've missed a pertinent detail. Lowering my gaze, I discover a black pistol in Kitty's hand.

"What are you doing?" I ask, internally cursing my broken leg and my inability to move quickly enough to help.

"Nuh-uh-uh." Kitty stops me when I take a step around the kitchen island. She jabs the gun into Stella's side, eliciting a yelp from her. "Wrong question. Ask me what I want?"

I don't want to piss her off at this very moment, so I play along. "What do you want, Kitty?"

She fires back quickly, already primed and ready with her demands. "I want $100k and for you to pay for Fox's rehab. He needs help, and you've been too busy putting your dick in my mouth to have the common courtesy to ask how your partner and dad's dearest friend is doing. Have you fucking seen him lately?"

"Yeah, last time I saw him was two days ago, Kitty, but you're the problem in that equation, not me. Stop giving him pills." I narrow my eyes.

"You don't seem to have a problem when I'm helping source your little problems too." Kitty snaps back, calling out my tendency to use narcotics more than I should.

"What's the $100k for?" I have to know.

"I'm going to Mexico and living large." She's delusional if she thinks she's going to survive in Mexico for very long with that little cash.

"Fair enough." There's no sense in arguing with an irrational person. "Okay. Lower the weapon, and I'll work on putting the money together. Nobody has to get hurt here."

Just as the words leave my mouth, my good leg is pulled out from underneath me. I land hard on my side, grunting in pain when a sharp ache shoots through my broken leg. I'm slow to respond to Darren crawling on top of me, taking too long to gather my bearings. He throws his fist into my face a few times, knocking me off kilter before I can pull myself together.

"Stop it!" Stella shouts, but she's no longer across the room. She's on Darren's back, slapping at his head. "Leave him alone!"

Darren rolls off me, dodges a few of Stella's attempted punches, and tackles her to the floor. They end up between the kitchen and living room, him straddling her body and choking her. I force myself off the floor and to head to Stella as quickly as I can.

Kitty flies from my right and jumps on top of my back, knocking me off balance and into the kitchen island. I yelp in pain, but I don't stop trying to get away.

"Stella!" I scream at her as I see her grip on Darren's hands start to weaken.

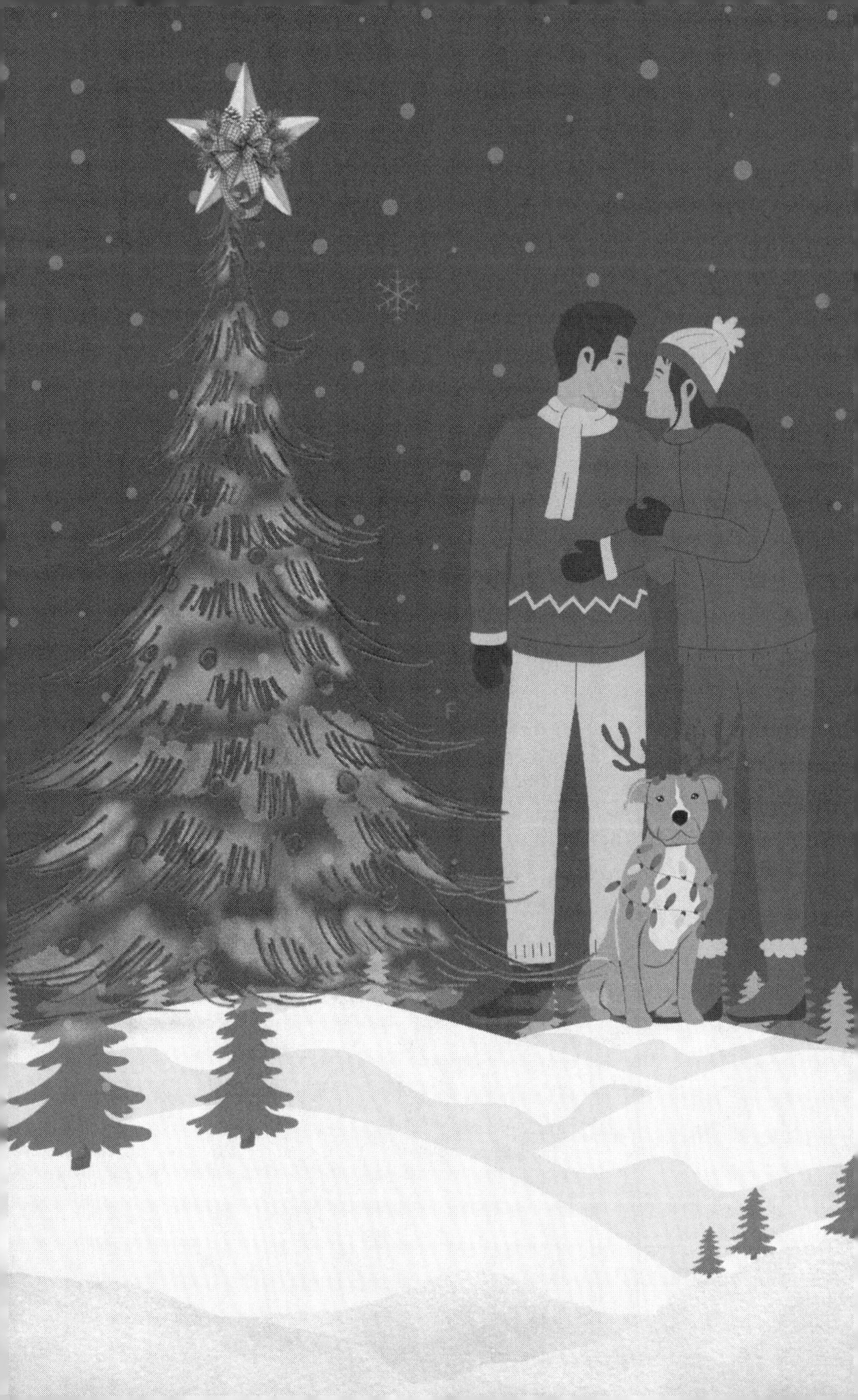

Chapter Nineteen

Stella

Darren's hands tighten around my neck a sliver more, causing me to lose the strength I need to fight him back. Slapping at his hands, arms, and face, I make one last final attempt to keep him from strangling the life out of me. But my vision begins to fade at the edges, and my heart beats rapidly in my ears.

As everything else blurs, I home in on the piece of mistletoe hanging above Darren and me – the one Kash hung a few days ago — and I make my last wish. Even this close to unconsciousness, I know there's no sense in using it to save myself.

Conjuring the image of him next to his twinkling tree, I focus on the smile he wore. I hope and wish he meets a woman who gives him the best Christmases of his life - full of trains, lights, hot chocolate, and mistletoe wishes. And, if I'm lucky enough, he'll remember me when he packs and unpacks the village each year.

A loud bang barely registers in my brain, and it's followed by snarling. I'm vaguely aware of Darren falling to the side. My vision is still blurry, but I roll over, coughing and gasping for air. Tears roll down my face as I struggle to take in oxygen, fighting to stay alive so I can return to the present.

Turning my head toward the back door, I can just make out the image of Kash's previous assistant. She's holding a long, skinny object I recognize as a shotgun when she racks a round. A blue pit bull sits beside her, just barely holding its shit together.

When my sight finally returns, the scene unfolds before me. Darren is a few feet away from me, holding his hands in the air like the criminal he really is. Kitty is face down on the ground, covering her blonde head with her long arms.

"I'm a police officer." Darren reaches inside of his black leather jacket to produce his badge. He lifts it into the air and points to me. "She's a fugitive on the run from Atlanta PD."

Kash reaches me, pulling my back to his chest, and wraps his arm around my middle. He snorts. "She's on the run from him," he tells Matilda. "Do us all a favor and light his ass up."

Matilda sneers at the information, and her dog doesn't take it too kindly either, lunging forward a step but stopping when his owner calls out to him. "Cricket, not yet."

Cricket the pit bull licks his chops and whines in protest, but he moves backward a few steps toward Matilda.

"This here's Mistletoe Creek, and we believe in pit bulls and pew pews. Cricket's two seconds away from eating your ass unless you start telling some truths, and if I don't like what you say, I'm gonna start shootin'." Matilda uses the end of her shot gun to motion for Darren to stand up. "Up ... slowly. If you make any sudden movements, I can't promise Cricket won't rip your pecker off."

Darren rises, his gaze flicking between her weapon and Cricket. Kitty sneaks through the living room. Matilda follows her with the barrel of her gun. "Not so fast, heifer."

Darren dives for his discarded gun, and Cricket takes that as his cue to inflict maximum damage, latching onto my ex's wrist and dragging him across the kitchen toward Matilda. He screams bloody murder at the top of his lungs, begging for help, but no one moves a finger to assist him.

Sirens wail in the distance while Cricket enjoys Darren as a chew toy. The ferocious dog shakes his head back and forth while playing tug of war with his body. Kash slides us both away from the bloodshed, protectively holding me to his chest.

Mistletoe Creek Police Department bursts through the door with their guns drawn, aiming in every direction. They aren't sure who are the bad guys in this scenario. When it's clear Matilda is in charge, they defer to her to take away Cricket's toy.

"We can't arrest him if the dog eats him." A man in the crowd says, stepping forward and cringing when Darren releases another scream.

Kash and I gather ourselves from the floor and get the hell out of the way. He guides me to the far side of the kitchen and softly whispers for me to climb onto the countertop. When his blue eyes land on my neck, I know Darren did visible damage ... again. Both concern and anger settle over his handsome features while he inspects the rest of me, but he doesn't utter a word for a long time.

When he's certain I'm fairly okay, he leans his forehead against mine, closes his blue eyes, and sighs. "He doesn't know how lucky he is that Cricket got to him first."

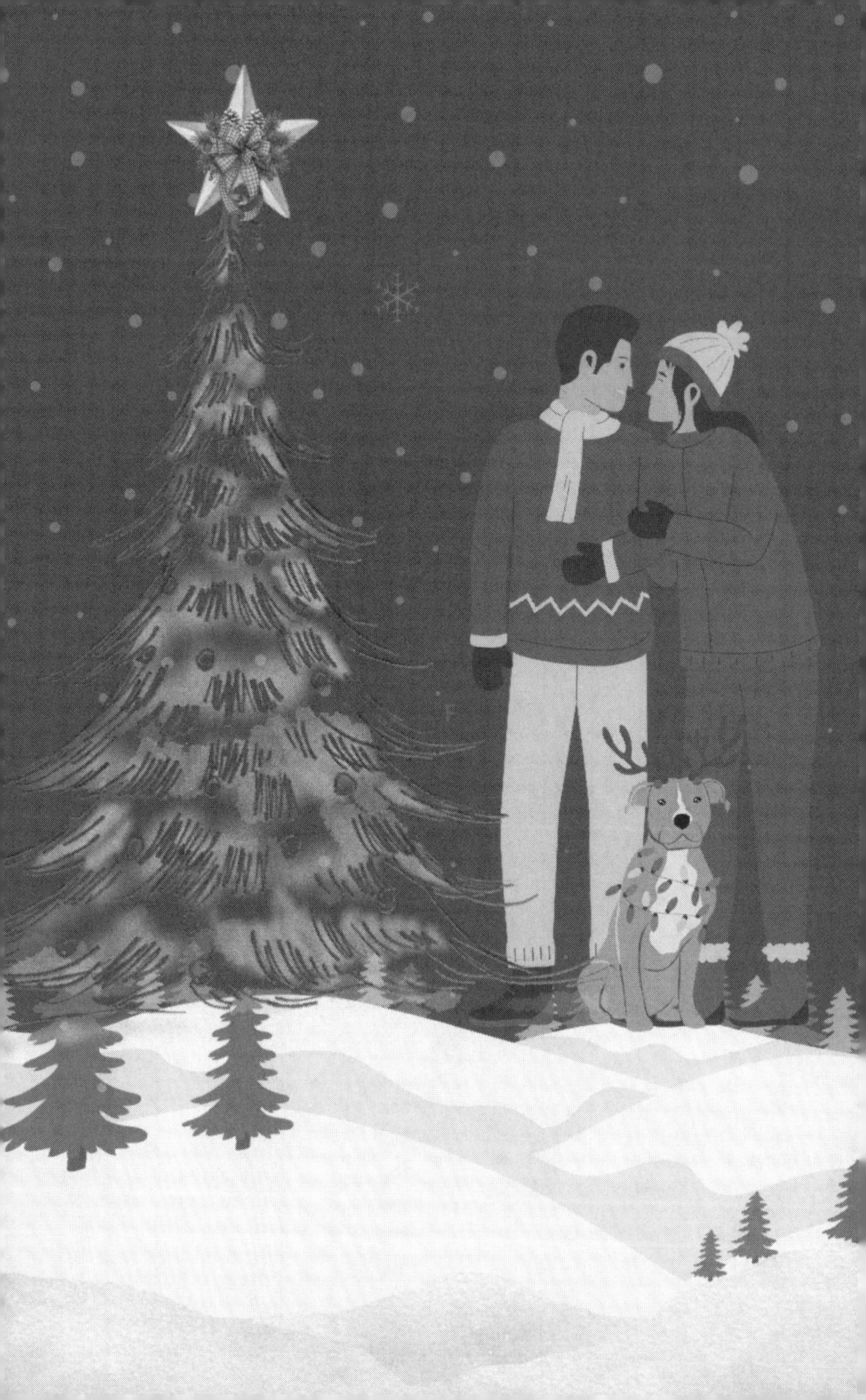

Chapter Twenty
Kash

The days directly after Darren and Kitty are arrested are filled with cold, icy rain. The weather reflects my mood as I wait for the inevitable to happen – Stella leaving me and this town in her rearview. For hours, I've stared at the village she pieced together herself, and I know I'll never put it up again, not without her.

The moments I spent watching her bring it to life are attached to the memory of her skin against my lips, the scent of her hair, and the way her body moved against mine. Her moans are on a constant replay in my mind. I desperately want to hear them again just to see if my memory even does them justice.

Today is Christmas Eve and the first day since I brought her home from the emergency room that I've given her space to think and be alone. I've circled her like a hawk as much as I can with a broken leg, keeping a close eye on her emotional state and the bruises on her neck. Every time I see the motley of colors on her throat, I'm tempted to break into the Mistletoe Creek City Jail and set Cricket loose on Darren all over again.

I don't know what I would've done if Matilda and Cricket hadn't stopped by Sunday morning to commandeer a string of Christmas lights. If she hadn't thought to grab her trusty shot gun when she heard Darren's weapon discharge, I don't know if everyone would've made it out alive.

A knock comes at the back door when the sun begins to set over Mistletoe Creek. My heart leaps into my throat with excitement, hoping like hell it's Stella. I haven't heard from her since she ventured to the garage apartment this morning.

Ambling as quickly as I can toward the kitchen door, I happily discover her on the other side drenched from the weather.

I wrench the door open. "Come in before you freeze to death."

"It is pretty cold out here," she admits before stepping inside beside me.

Gazing down at her, it becomes clear to me she's been crying. Her eyes are red and swollen. The whites are bloodshot. Normally, I'd completely ignore it, considering her emotional state is none of my business. But what if I want it to be? What if it already is?

"Have you eaten? I can make us a salad or a grilled cheese." I offer dinner since I'm worried she hasn't had a meal all day. I'm also avoiding the conversation I'm dreading having with her.

"No, thank you. I had a protein bar earlier." She's been a tad bit blue all week.

I close the back door and make the only thing I can think of to cheer her up – a mug of hot chocolate. "Have a seat." I point to a bar stool at the kitchen island.

She waits for me to move away before she climbs onto it. I move incredibly fast for a dude with a casted leg. I also keep a steady eye on her as she fidgets with her hands, turning them over and frowning like they offended her.

When the cocoa beeps in the microwave, I ask for her help. "Would you mind carrying these over there for me?"

It snaps her out of her thoughts. "Of course. It smells good." Even her excitement falls flat.

I follow her to the island, opting to stand instead of sit. As I lean my crutches against it, my doorbell rings.

"I'll get it." She's up before I can stop her, but my anxiety skyrockets over her answering the door without me.

What the hell is going on with me? I sleep with her one time, and I'm losing my mind over her answering the door.

"Where is that bastard?" Branson Rutgers' voice travels to my ears.

Gathering my crutches, I curse myself for not being able to run to Stella's side. "You can't come in!" she shouts at him.

As I round the corner to the living room, Rutgers is storming past Stella, knocking into her shoulder as he slips inside. Stella loses her balance, falling into the open door. She yelps in pain when she lands on her ass.

A memory dislodges from my early years, and I finally know exactly who she reminds me of — my mother. They don't favor each other, but it's the quiet strength they both possess. As old images from another life passes behind my eyes, the night before my mom was murdered by my stepfather consumes me for a moment.

My beautiful mother gathers me into her tiny lap, her kind voice warming me all over. "Everything will be better soon, my sweet boy. We're going to a new place where we don't have to be afraid anymore."

"Where are we going, mommy?" I ask, hoping we never have to see my stepfather again.

He's a mean man. He smells bad, and he hits my mommy. I don't like when he makes her cry.

She pulls me tighter against her bosom, rocking us back and forth. "Somewhere we can be safe and happy, sweetheart."

"Can I be a real boy there?" I've always wanted to be more like the boys at school.

"You're already a real boy, Kashton. Who said you weren't?" Concern weighs heavily in her tone.

Afraid her husband will hear me, I whisper. "Randy gets mad when I cry. I try not to, mommy, but he hurts me."

She tenses around me, not saying a word for the longest time. "How does he hurt you, sweet boy?" When I don't reply for fear she'll think I'm not a real boy too, she begins to sing "Wish Upon a Star" from my favorite movie – Pinocchio. "I hope all of your dreams come true, Kashton."

I never uttered the words to my mom, but she knew what Randy had done. She was willing to take every beating he dealt her, but she wasn't standing for anyone hurting her son. My mother died defending me. She lost her life because she confronted him, finding her inner strength through her anger, but it wasn't a match for Randy's drunken rage. The moment Rutgers knocked Stella down, the look of protective fierceness formed on her face. It's the same expression my mother wore when she told Randy she was prosecuting him for his crimes, moments before he snapped her neck.

Stella tenderly stands from the floor, not checking herself for injuries, and she goes right after Rutgers. "I said you can't come in here!"

"Shut up, bitch," Rutgers viciously replies over his shoulder. He doesn't see me round the corner and runs straight into my chest.

I look down at him, towering over his small stature. "What did you just call her?"

He bounces off my body and takes a step back, glaring up at me. "This is between you and me." Waving a white letter in the air, he continues, "What's this bullshit about you withdrawing as my counsel? I paid you a small fortune, and for what?"

Leaning forward, I place a finger over his lips. "Shhhhh, little man." I pat him on his head. "Let me explain." I crack my neck on both sides, preparing for my delivery. "You're a fucking asshole. Plain and simple. I don't like you. You hit your wife. And maybe worse. Your stepson is terrified of you. They're both miserable. You are one of the most unlikeable people I've ever met. I'm not in the business of representing wife beaters or child abusers. I'm withdrawing as your attorney. You'll need to find other representation. So that's what the letter says that I sent." I've tried to be nice and professional in my written correspondence, but he crossed a line by showing up at my house and hurting Stella, which I'm not going to let slide, simply because it wasn't an accident.

Rutgers' face turns a concerning shade of red as he sputters. He can't form a coherent sentence. He's lost control. I can't be controlled by his fist or his money, and people like him don't do so well with losing their precious power.

Using the crutches to close the small space between us, I let one of them fall away. While he's focused on that, I use my free hand to wrap around his throat. "This is your warning, Branson. If you ever put your hands on Stella, or any person for that matter, I'm coming after you. There's no amount of money you'll be able to throw at me to make me go away."

His feeble attempt at pulling my fingers from around his neck is laughable, so I squeeze a hair more. I want to see the panic in his eyes before I release him, so he knows I'm not fucking around. I will hunt him down and stomp a mud hole in his ass if he harms a hair on any soul's head.

"Do we understand each other?" I speak slowly, enunciating each word, just so there's no miscommunication.

Rutgers doesn't immediately reply. He's a stubborn little psychopath. Smirking, I tighten my grip more, lifting an expectant brow. He can suffocate for all I give a fuck. Just when I think he'll pass out, he taps at my forearm.

It's cute he thinks he can tap out.

"I asked you a question," I remind him.

He nods vigorously as his face turns a purple shade of red.

I release him. "I need words, shit for brains."

Bending at the waist, he takes big heaping gulps of breaths, but he doesn't respond.

I become impatient. Pulling him up by his sandy brown hair, I slap him on the cheek. "Are you good?"

Tears pour down his face, and I find probably too much happiness in them.

"I understand." It's barely coherent.

"Good. Now apologize to Stella and get the fuck out of here." I let go and give him five seconds to recover before moving to the door, in case he's forgotten where it is.

I almost kick him in the ass when he walks through it, mumbling an apology, but I'm scared I'd lose my balance again. Slamming it shut and locking the deadbolt, I turn back to check on Stella. Her eyes are shiny with tears.

"You're hurt." My entire being aches at her being harmed by anything or anyone. "I'm going to fucking kill him."

"No," she replies to me as I turn back toward the door. "I'm okay."

Closing the space between us as quickly as I can manage, I'm again reminded of my poor mom. She'd finally gained the courage to leave a terrible man, but her time was cut short before she got her shot at happiness. Stopping underneath the mistletoe I hung between the kitchen and living room, I immediately know what I want to use my wish for – Stella's happiness.

I wish for her total happiness – to be loved and treated like a good woman should. I hope she finds her soulmate to give her hot chocolate, Christmas villages, and mistletoe wishes. But more than that, I hope she finds her home – a place where she's loved, appreciated, and a physical space that's her very own.

Tears prick my own eyes, because I know what comes next. She's going to leave because the case is over. With Darren in jail, she has the freedom to start over and reinvent herself however she pleases. Part of me is excited for her, but the other part of me will miss her. Missing any woman other than Matilda is foreign to me. The center of my chest tightens and aches at the mere thought of seeing Stella's taillights leaving Mistletoe Creek.

"Why the tears?" I ask her, more so because I want to know how to fix it.

She swallows hard and looks down at her feet. "I'll miss this place."

"Don't leave on Christmas." I don't even care that I'm begging. Anyone in earshot can hear the plea in my voice.

"Tomorrow is Christmas." Her tone is low and sad.

Pride comes before the fall, so I move past it. I take a leap of faith, knowing rejection is likely. "I'm asking you to spend Christmas with me."

Her eyes lift to mine, and they're full of disbelief.

Before she can object, I play the only card I'm holding, my words rushing out before I can stop them. "I have a gift for you."

"For me?" She's surprised.

"Yeah, of course, for you." I grow more nervous by the second as I wait for her to respond.

"Okay. Thank you. You didn't have to buy me a present though." Pure shame tugs at her features. "I didn't get you anything. I'm sorry, I didn't know —"

I interrupt her. "You built the best Christmas village known to man, and it's right here in my living room." I motion toward the fireplace before dropping my hand and resting my gaze back on her. "And you gave me you, Stella," I say in a quiet tone.

I let her soak in my words, hoping she understands she quickly came to mean something to me. I'm not sure what that is, but I know I want to be a better person because of her.

"The only issue with your gift is it won't be here until tomorrow. I scheduled for a Christmas Day delivery." I bite the inside of my cheek, nervously anticipating her rejection.

"I was going to hit the road tonight." She looks away, fidgeting with the sleeve on her black hoodie.

"Can you stay until tomorrow?" God, I sound pathetic, even to my own ears.

Finally, she puts me out of my misery and nods. "Sure. If you'll have me, I'd love to stay another night."

She still won't give me her gaze, so I take a step toward her, tuck her chin between my finger and thumb, and do my absolute best to refrain from kissing her.

"I have Hallmark cued on the TV." I attempt to entice her to spend a few hours with me. I've missed her all day.

She gives me a small smile. "Anything good coming on?"

"You'd have to look. They leave off the cheese ratings." I laugh.

"I require a rating of four out of five on the cheese-o-meter." Her smile grows wider.

"Psh. It's Hallmark. I'm sure whatever we turn on will meet your high standards." I tease.

We move to the couch – her on one side and me on the other. I endure my second Hallmark movie of my life, but it isn't so bad. I actually get into the movie and hyper focus on the plot. It's cheesy as fuck and unrealistic, but it makes Stella happy. She's been unusually quiet and still for the last twenty minutes, so I check on her.

"Did you pass out first at the party?" I nudge her with my foot.

She doesn't move.

"She's sleeping," I say to the room.

I leave her just like she is, covering her with a blanket and returning to the movie to find out the ending, but it doesn't stop me from glancing at her every few minutes in adoration.

Just before I close my eyes, I think of my mother again. Smiling, I wish upon the star sitting atop my tree that all my dreams will come true, and that fate will guide my biggest desire to stay in Mistletoe Creek.

What the hell could it hurt?

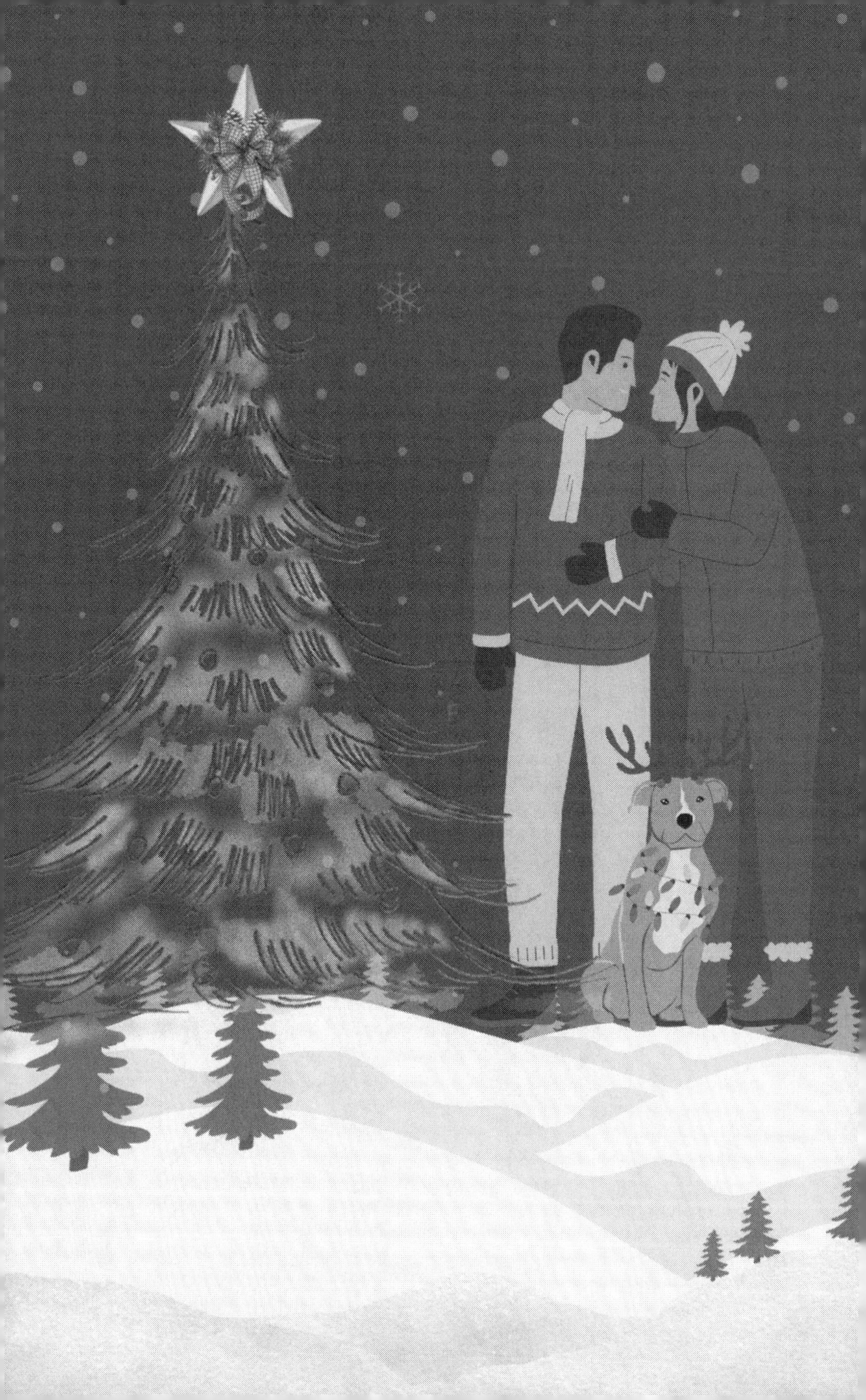

Chapter Twenty-One
Stella

The scent of bacon and coffee fill my nose seconds before I open my eyes. Peeking between my lids, I check to see if Kash is still at the other end of the couch.

"Rise and shine, sleeping beauty." His deep voice scares the hell out of me.

Refocusing right in front of me, I zero in on his crotch first. It should be illegal for men who look like him to wear gray sweatpants. When he clears his throat, I lift my gaze higher.

He's smirking and holding a black mug of coffee out to me. "I thought you'd enjoy this since we haven't had any in several days."

I blink in disbelief. This isn't the same man who was standing butt ass naked in his kitchen, pissing in his dishwasher.

"Thank you." I accept the drink after sitting up. I look through the windows. "What time is it?"

"A little after ten." His crotch is now eye level, so his reply barely registers.

"Hmmm. I slept all night." It's unusual for me to sleep through the night.

"I imagine you feel safe now that Darren is locked away?" he asks as he has a seat beside me.

"For the first time in … maybe my entire life, I can breathe a little easier," I admit, not discounting the anxiety about the unknown direction of my life now. I have no clue which direction I want to point my car when I leave Mistletoe Creek. The freedom of going anywhere in the world with no one to object makes my soul soar. "Is that bacon frying?"

His eyes grow wide before he springs from the couch, once again forgetting about his leg. "Fuck!"

"I'll get it." I leap from my seat and round the corner to the kitchen. Pulling the pan of bacon off the hot burner, I flip on the exhaust fan on the hood. The charred black pieces continue to crackle and pop on the stove, because the grease is too hot. A drop of grease splatters against the top of my hand. Shaking out the burn, I rush to the sink. "Holy shit, it hurts!"

Kash ambles in, moving as fast as he can, and stops behind me. He's so tall, looking over my shoulder isn't an issue for him. "I'll get ice." Seconds later, he reaches around me, handing me a large cube, and says, "I'll be right back."

While he's gone, I press the ice to my hand to cool the burn more quickly than tap water will. The sting begins to subside by the time he returns with a first aid kit tucked under one arm. Rushing to help him, I take it and place it on the island countertop. I unlatch the lid and open it, hoping he has nonstick bandages and petroleum jelly.

He swats me away from the kit. "Let me help."

"You're on crutches," I argue.

"Humor me." He casts a smirk over his shoulder. "I believe there's burn ointment in the kit." He sifts through different types of supplies and lifts a small foil packet into the air. "Good, it's here." Patting the countertop, he motions for me to have a seat on it. "I can doctor you better up here."

I lift myself onto the island and stick out my burnt hand.

He steps between my legs and pulls my hand into his. "You can relax it." Kash removes what's left of the ice, gently pats it dry, applies ointment, and tapes a bandage around it. "All done." His blue eyes lift to mine. "Is it stinging any less yet?"

"A little." My voice is quiet because he's standing so close.

God, how beautiful can one man be? And when did Kashton Saint become a compassionate, caring person?

His dark hair and clothes are rumpled from sleep. He smells like bacon and coffee, and everything I imagined Christmas morning would be when I grew up and fell in love with my soulmate. He's disheveled, and yet, still so handsome. I can't handle the tattoos, insane muscles, and him looking like he's been freshly fucked all at the same time. My poor brain might explode. My ovaries certainly will.

He reaches out, tenderly pushing my hair behind my ear, but never lifts his gaze from mine. Leaning down and in, he presses his soft lips to mine. The moment his tongue touches mine, I moan and his follows – a deep, guttural sound of pleasure which makes my toes curl. I'm so lost to him I don't completely register the doorbell ringing.

Kash breaks the kiss and curses. "*Fuck*. I forgot." He cradles my face in both of his hands, like I might fly away if he's not looking, and places a sweet peck on me. "If this wasn't important, I wouldn't bother answering the door. And I just want you to know that before I walk away. Okay?"

"Okay?" I ask more than answer, because he's not making any sense.

He nods with finality and kisses me again, pausing like he might deepen it, but ultimately decides to answer the door. "Don't come in here yet. Please," he says to me over his shoulder as he walks in the other direction.

I slide off the island.

There's a commotion a few moments later which consists of Matilda yelling and a puppy yapping. "You little shit!"

Kash laughs and shouts, "Incoming!"

A blue pit bull puppy gallops into the kitchen, jumping on my legs and wagging its tail. I scoop the baby up, and it attacks me with kisses before I can have a look at its face. "Aren't you adorable?" I manage between being licked.

Matilda and Kash join us, smiling at me and the puppy.

"Cute pup," I say to Matilda.

"I'm glad you think so. He's Cricket's son. Well, I hate to run, but I have to speed over to my daughter's before her mother-in-law arrives and tries to cook again. If we don't stop her before she ruins the entire meal, we'll all be starving at dinner." She shakes her head, exasperated and hurried, before hugging Kash. I'm surprised when she includes me in her affection, also wrapping me and the puppy in a warm embrace. She darts out of the room, waving off Kash's offer to walk her to the door. "No, no. Stay. Enjoy Christmas, you two!"

The door slams as Kash makes his way over to me and the puppy. "I haven't seen him in person yet." Petting the little guy, his eyes are full of happiness.

"You got a dog you haven't met yet?" I quirk a brow at him.

Kash leans in to whisper into my ear. "Check his collar." He doesn't back up, remaining right next to my ear. His breath tickles the area just below it.

I check the collar, which I haven't noticed until now, and find a small, green velvet ring box attached to a string. "What do you have here?" I ask the precious little darling in my arms.

Opening the box, I find a bronze key and a little scroll of paper.

Stay with me.

Love,

Kash

"Please," he pleads.

Tears immediately prick my eyes as overwhelming emotions wash over me, and within seconds, they roll down my cheeks. "I can't," I sob.

"Why not?" He backs away enough to give me more breathing room. There's also moisture in his eyes.

My overactive mind goes into overdrive with the reasons rolling off my tongue. "I can't stay because I don't have a job. I need a job to afford a place to live. It's hard to find a decent-paying job when I'm living out of my ca—"

"You have a job —" he begins, but I cut him off.

"No. I can't even take the ten thousand dollars you offered because I didn't work the case. It's worth it just to hear you withdrew as his counsel."

"You most certainly will. And you can work with me on more cases, so the job problem is solved." The plea is written all over his face.

"I can't work for you. I've seen you naked." More than once.

He blinks at me. "Baby, I've been inside of you. You've more than seen me naked."

I glance away. Fair point, but I'm not conceding. I can't stay in Mistletoe Creek because Kash is here. We've slept together. I've seen him turn over a new leaf in areas of his life, making better decisions about other people's best interests. It makes him wildly attractive to me. But knowing what he sounds like when he falls apart inside of me isn't something a woman just gets over. It's not something I'll ever forget either. "I'll never be able to have a conversation with you as we pass each other in town weeks or months from now and pretend like I don't know what my name sounds like rolling off your tongue."

A long, pregnant pause stretches between us before he reaches up and pushes my hair behind my other ear. "Good. I want to be *the one* calling out your name, Stella."

"And I can't work cases with you because you represent low-lifes," I sputter.

"Perfect." He leans down and places a kiss on my forehead. "I've already changed the focus of the firm. We're no longer representing bullshit cases. We'll specialize in foster care cases, adoption cases, and domestic abuse cases. We don't represent assholes anymore. We'll write grants and empower Mistletoe Creek's domestic abuse victims to obtain legal counsel and other resources needed to stay safe."

"When did you decide this?" I ask, hoping it isn't an insane effort to keep me in Mistletoe Creek.

He presses a kiss to my forehead once more and takes the ring box from me. "When I decided to give you the key to my heart."

Remembering the key, I watch him pluck it from the velvet box and put it all together. *The Hallmark movie.*

A gasp and a sob leave me.

"You're only the second woman I've given it to. The first one left me before her time." For the first time since we met, there's shyness resting in his eyes.

"Your mom?" I ask to be sure.

"Yeah." He chances another look at me, and from the looks of him, he's just as scared as I am of even considering handing over my heart to him.

His answer pulls at my heartstrings. "I'm broken," I whisper. "I'm not who you want."

"That's what Pip Squeak is for." He points to the dog.

"What?" I'm so confused.

"He's here to make sure no one else hurts you while I put all of your beautifully broken pieces back together." He's looking at me with an emotion I haven't had directed at me since my grandfather was alive – love.

Thinking back to my mistletoe wish a few days ago, I try hard to reconcile me being Kash's person — the woman I wish will make him happy and see how much potential he really has. I've settled my entire life and ignored a lot of red flags, but I've never been afraid to fall in love. Yet, I'm afraid to admit I already have deep feelings for him. They developed quickly and without warning.

"You're overthinking." He pulls me from my thoughts.

"Yes," I admit and swallow past the lump of emotion in my throat.

"Don't do that." He snickers, but it sounds a tad nervous. "Look —"

He halts his sentence when he takes the puppy from me, sets him on the floor, and returns to me. His hand dives into my hair as his lips land on mine. Another hand dances down my spine and settles on my hip, which he uses to pull me closer. Diving into me, he kisses me like I've never been kissed. My ovaries high-five each other. My toes curl. My hoo-hah quivers, and by God, I kiss him back like I've never kissed anyone.

Breaking the kiss, he murmurs against my lips. "Give us a chance, Stella."

Pip Squeak whines as if supporting Kash's statement.

"You hush," I talk back to the dog, then I let Kash have the business. "Nobody told you to stop kissing me."

Mistletoe Creek Series

Experience All Titles in the Mistletoe Creek Series

Robbing from Mistletoe
Once Upon a Frosty Winter: A Small Town, Misunderstood Grumpy Holiday Romance
Midnight in Mistletoe
Wicked Love
Say My Name
All Snowed Gin: A Small Town, Grumpy/Sunshine Holiday Romance
Taming Mistletoe: A Childhood Best-Friends to Lovers Romance
Entangled

Also By Sasha Marshall

Experience Sasha's Other Titles
The Guitar Face Series
Broken
There's No Crying in Rock-N-Roll
Walking Back to Georgia
River of Deceit
Make It Rain
There's a Woman

The Second Down Series
False Start

Standalone Books
The Fire Witch: A Zvi Jayden

Short Story
Wild Side

About the Author

Award-winning and best-selling author SASHA MARSHALL is devoted to giving her readers humorous adventures with a love story sure to melt their hearts—and their minds. She wants you to laugh, cry, get angry, and sigh when you find redemption in a story because that's the roller coaster of real life. Her knowledge of the music industry comes from being a touring concert photographer with legendary bands such as The Allman Brothers Band and others she met along the way. A self-proclaimed free spirit, she's most often found outdoors, capturing a photograph, people watching, or reading a book. Sasha makes her home in the beautiful state of Georgia and loves to hear from her readers. Visit her website at SashaMarshall.com